Darcy and Anne

JUDITH BROCKLEHURST

SOURCEBOOKS LANDMARK™
AN IMPRINT OF SOURCEBOOKS, INC.®
NAPERVILLE, ILLINOIS

Published by Sourcebooks Landmark, an imprint of Sourcebooks, Inc.
P.O. Box 4410, Naperville, Illinois 60567–4410
(630) 961–3900
FAX: (630) 961–2168
www.sourcebooks.com

Library of Congress Cataloging-in-Publication Data

Brocklehurst, Judith.
  Darcy and Anne / Judith Brocklehurst.
     p. cm.
  1. Darcy, Fitzwilliam (Fictitious character)--Fiction. 2. Bennet, Elizabeth (Fictitious character)--Fiction. 3. England--Social life and customs--19th century--Fiction. I. Austen, Jane, 1775-1817. Pride and prejudice. II. Title.
  PS3602.R626D37 2009
  813'.6--dc22

                              2009019074

Printed and bound in the United States of America
CHG 10 9 8 7 6 5 4 3 2 1

For Brian
with love

Chapter 1

Lady Catherine de Bourgh to Mr Fitzwilliam Darcy

My dear Nephew,

The disagreement between us regarding your marriage has gone on long enough. I disapproved; but that is in the past.

I am convinced that, after two years at Pemberley, your wife has become a worthy representative of our family. I am supported in this view by a letter from my old friend, Lady Louisa Benton, who lives, as you know, in your part of the world. Lady Louisa tells me that at a reception she recently attended, "your pretty niece, Mrs Darcy" was dressed with taste and elegance, and much admired for her ease of manner and witty conversation.

Let us let bygones be bygones. Her want of family connections is no longer a consideration; a wife, after all, takes the rank of her husband. The fact of her sister's disgraceful elopement with the son of your father's steward is known to no one in our set, except myself, and I shall never mention it outside the family. I have re-considered; I have made my resolution; I shall visit you.

Our visit will take place very soon, for another circumstance has arisen: Mrs Jenkinson, Anne's companion, has left us. She has actually taken a position as a governess, in the family of a rich manufacturer with three small children, and they say she receives twice the salary that I was paying her, has a fire in her bedroom, and dines with the family every day! They are lowborn, and I suppose they like to say that their governess has been in a nobleman's family. Be that as it may, we can find no one to replace her. I have decided: Anne must marry. She is full old enough; she mopes here, and marriage will lift her spirits and give her an interest. I shall expect her husband to live with us here; indeed I shall insist on it; and we shall go on exactly as we do now, except that we will not need a paid companion.

However, I can find no young man, nor indeed any man, in this neighbourhood, to marry her. I am acquainted with several families of sufficient station who have sons, but whenever I invite them here, they are already engaged, or just going to town, or there is sickness in the family. When we pay a morning visit, the young men are always out about the place, or riding, or hunting; we visit with the mother and father, and it gets us nowhere. As for billiard rooms, they should be banned by law; the young men get into them, and cannot be got out. We need a larger neighbourhood; we need new acquaintances. I think you will admit, my dear nephew, that by marrying as you did, you have put me in the position, which I did not expect, of having to find a husband for my daughter, and you ought to assist us by every means in your power. We shall visit you and stay until Anne has formed an eligible connection.

You will know which men, among your acquaintance, are fit to marry the daughter of Sir Lewis de Bourgh, and your wife will easily be able to arrange a series of pleasant little entertainments to get them to the house. I do not object to an older man, or to a widower, and I do not insist on a title, provided he be of sufficient rank and means, and cognizant, of course, of the honour of marrying into a family such as ours. Once matters are satisfactorily arranged, we shall all remove to Rosings for the wedding; and—I am quite determined, it is time—your wife shall be of the party.

We start from here the day after tomorrow, and will be on the road by the time this letter reaches you. I do not know when we shall reach Pemberley; we must travel slowly, as Anne gets queasy after an hour or two in the chaise.

Believe me still to be, my dear Nephew,

Your affectionate Aunt,

C. de Bourgh.

By the by, Mrs Collins was brought to bed three days ago. The child is a boy, and Mr Collins is half killed with delight, so that he makes even less sense than usual. It is very inconvenient for me, for they cannot come to dinner, and with Mrs Jenkinson gone, we have been obliged to sit down alone. However, I visited and was shown the infant. It is a very ugly child, but then Mrs Collins has no pretension to beauty. As for Mr Collins, when I sought an incumbent for the living of Hunsford, I made sure not to get a good-looking man, for a handsome parson is fit for nothing but to put ideas into the young women's heads.

C de B.

Chapter 2

ON A FINE DAY, IN AN OPEN CARRIAGE, TRAVELLING IS ONE OF life's most pleasant experiences. But if the day be hot, the carriage closed, and the traveller crowded, the pleasure is much diminished. And should the traveller be not at all eager to arrive at the destination, the journey is misery indeed.

On a warm day of early summer, a post-chaise was proceeding at a good pace towards Pemberley, in Derbyshire. The bulky dress of Lady Catherine de Bourgh took up most of the seat, for Lady Catherine did not approve of the modern fashions, so that Anne de Bourgh was obliged to share rather less than half of the space with her mother's maid. She wondered if Mullins was feeling as hot and wretched as she was, but for half a lifetime Mullins had been Lady Catherine's sewing maid, and, recently promoted to be her personal maid, she never ventured any opinion. She was vinegar-faced, dour, and silent. You would never know what Mullins thought, or felt.

But there was no doubt as to Lady Catherine's mood. At the posting-house where they had stayed the night before, a violent illness, probably from bad meat, had laid low several people, mostly servants, and including their coachman and both of the footmen. Lady Catherine was very angry, and had refused to spend another night in the inn. She would go on without her servants, she said; they were within twenty miles of Pemberley, and would arrive there well within the day. The servants should bring the coach on when they were recovered.

A post-chaise was hired. It was the handsomest that could be obtained, and actually was travelling much faster than the family carriage, but a hired post-chaise is not a barouche. Even had one been available for hire, nothing could make up for the fact that they must arrive at Pemberley, they must drive through Lambton and up the approach, in a vehicle that did not carry the de Bourgh family crest on its panels, and no one would know who was arriving. Lady Catherine was not in a good temper.

Anne, on the other hand, in spite of her discomfort, was by no means in a hurry to arrive at Pemberley. She did not think she could ever be comfortable there. Anne had a pretty good idea of the content of her mother's letter, and could well imagine the feelings of its recipient. Her mother, she knew, could not imagine herself unwelcome anywhere, but Anne could anticipate the forced smiles, the resigned attitude, the careful attentions, all the more careful because unfelt, that would greet the arrival of such unwanted guests as they would be! Her distress was compounded by the thought that, wanted or unwanted, they must stay, and stay until a husband had been found for her! The thought of the stratagems her mother might employ to achieve such an end made her shudder.

And this must happen at Pemberley, where her hostess would be Mrs Darcy, the brilliant young woman who had snatched the great matrimonial prize, Mr Fitzwilliam Darcy, from Lady Catherine's grasp.

Anne was quite certain that Mrs Darcy despised her. She could never forget the very first evening they had met, when Mr and

Mrs Collins had brought their pretty, quick-tongued friend, Miss Elizabeth Bennet, to dinner at Rosings. Anne, who seldom felt well, had been bilious all day. By the evening, she had a severe head-ache, but neither she nor Mrs Jenkinson had said anything about it, for Lady Catherine disliked being reminded that her daughter was sickly—though she frequently alluded to the fact herself.

Poor Mrs Jenkinson, always afraid of losing her post, had fidg-eted desperately all through dinner, pressing Anne to take every dish, though she knew perfectly well that she could not eat anything. From time to time, Anne had tried to eat, but every mouthful, as soon as she had swallowed it, turned out to be exactly what was most likely to make her sick.

Dinner had seemed endless; and after dinner, Anne had been made to say what card game she would like to play. At random, her head throbbing, she had said, "Cassino"; she did not know why, for she did not like it. They had sat all evening playing, hardly speaking a word except as it affected the game. Miss Elizabeth Bennet, sitting there in the pretty white muslin dress that Lady Catherine said could not have cost more than six shillings the yard, had been perfectly polite, but she had clearly been very bored, and it was clear that she regarded it as Anne's fault—or so it seemed to poor Anne. Anne had never felt so plain, so sickly and stupid. She was sure that when she met Mrs Darcy again, she would feel exactly the same.

Life at Rosings had not been happy for Anne in recent years. She had loved her gentle, scholarly father. When she was a child, he had spent a great deal of time with her, telling her stories, and later he had formed her taste for reading, sharing with her the books he loved. She still grieved over his sudden, early death. Her mother had seen to it that his obsequies were magnificent, had paid for a very handsome monument, and had forgotten him.

Her happiest times were when she was alone, in her father's library, among the fossil curiosities and outdated books. She did not blame Mrs Jenkinson for leaving Rosings. In fact, though nobody knew it (and Anne shuddered, when she thought what her mother would say), she had encouraged her companion to apply for the post of governess in a rich family. Mrs Jenkinson was timid and kindly. She had been an excellent governess when Anne was a child, but she had no talent for instructing a grown woman, and for a couple of years, in fact, had been filling the post of a personal maid.

Anne had hoped that, if Mrs Jenkinson left, her mother would engage somebody who might take her a little further in piano and in French, and help her to read the more advanced authors, the geography and natural sciences that she loved. She did not think of asking to ride, to dance, or to sing, for she had always been told that her health did not permit these activities.

However, her mother had decided not to engage another companion for her, or even a maid: "Mullins will look after you. She has very little to do." Mullins had not been pleased. Almost all that Anne had heard from her, since Mrs Jenkinson left, was "I take my orders from Lady Catherine, miss," and "My lady has given no orders for that, miss." It was all Anne could do to get her clothes taken care of and her dress unlaced at the inns where they had stayed along the road.

Anne was constantly ill, and the medication provided by her mother's doctor did little to relieve, and nothing to cure her. It might have been assumed that her health would be found too poor for her to think of marriage, with its attendant dangers. But she was always told that her health was no cause for concern, she would soon be better, and then she was to marry her cousin Darcy. She was never asked whether she wanted to marry him, and her mother would have been astonished to know that, had she been asked, the answer would have been a frightened, but definite, "No."

Anne was afraid of him: his cold manner, his heavy silences, his sardonic looks, his dismissive remarks, above all the occasional witticisms, subtle and derogatory, that hurt her, but that her mother did not understand, or seem to notice.

He had been a splendid young man when she was scarcely more than a child; her mother's assertion that they had been in the cradle together was a myth of her mother's creating; he was the older by five years. He was handsome, he was rich, he was clever; but he had never paid any attention to her, and she knew that he did not want to marry her.

What a relief, when she heard he was to marry Miss Bennet! And what a surprise: for she was neither rich nor well connected. However, on thinking it over, Anne remembered not only how pretty Miss Bennet was, but how lively, how confident, and altogether charming!

When cousin Darcy was there, she had watched the two of them talk together—the enjoyment that had flashed like lightning between them. No stale, awkward nothings for them, no heavy silences! They had seemed almost to fence, like two swordsmen, but yet it was play. The bright-eyed young woman seemed never to be afraid, always on the verge of laughter.

Then there had been a strange evening, when the Collinses had come to drink tea, but Miss Bennet had not come with them, because, they said, she had the head-ache; Mrs Collins said she was very bad. "It must be bad indeed," Mr Collins had said, "to compel her to forgo the pleasure of drinking tea with the ladies of Rosings," as he bowed to Anne, in his usual ingratiating way.

Cousin Darcy had seemed unable to give his attention to anything. He was not speaking, walking up and down, in a restless, uncomfortable way that was not at all like him. Her mother, as usual, had noticed nothing; but then he had suddenly excused himself, and left the room, saying he must have some fresh air. "You have been out in the air all day, Darcy," her mother had called—but he was gone.

He had come back, an hour or so later, looking like thunder; no, worse than that—as if he had been hit over the head. He had taken no part in any conversation, seemed not to know that they were there, even, and left them very early, saying he must go to bed.

Early the next day, "Your cousin has gone," her mother had said. "I really began to think he could not bear to leave, he put it off so often. I am sure he will want to be a great deal at Rosings, when you are married." She had given no thought to his exit the previous evening, and had certainly not connected it to his sudden departure. But Mrs Collins's maid was the niece of Lady Catherine's cook at Rosings; indeed, the great lady herself had commanded Mrs Collins to employ her; and did she not think that tidings from the one household must perforce arrive at the other? Indeed, did she not know it? Had she herself not made use of the fact, many times, to keep the Parsonage under her all-seeing eye? By noon of that day, everyone in Hunsford knew that Mr Darcy, when he had left his aunt's house the evening before, had gone to the Parsonage. The sole exception was Lady Catherine, for nobody had dared to tell her.

They had not seen Cousin Darcy again. Then they heard that Miss Bennet was to marry him! Lady Catherine called her a vulgar, lowborn, hurly-burly village girl, who had schemed to entrap a wealthy man into marriage, and who had refused, even when Lady

Catherine herself had reasoned with her, to give him up! Anne could only feel gratitude, and admiration for Miss Bennet, who had not only accepted her terrifying cousin but had actually resisted Lady Catherine's bullying. Her mother's temper was frightening for several weeks, and Anne was on the receiving end of a good many unpleasant tirades. But most of her mother's anger was directed at the Collinses, and anything was better than the prospect of marrying Cousin Darcy.

Then Mrs Jenkinson had left, and Lady Catherine had discovered that it was not easy to hire a new companion. She needed somebody not too young—but not too old. It must be somebody presentable enough to dine with them, when there was no other company, or when a woman was needed to balance the table, but not a female relation, who would object to being banished to the schoolroom when she was not wanted, as if she were a servant. An extra woman, on the days when they dined alone, was no asset at all!

In short, what Lady Catherine needed was not a gentlewoman, but a gentleman. Anne must marry. Since Cousin Darcy was unavailable, she must marry somebody else.

So had begun a new and humiliating period, as Anne was dragged to balls and assemblies in outmoded dresses with large thick skirts, for Lady Catherine called the new high-waisted styles immodest: the Queen, she pointed out, did not allow the Royal Princesses to wear them. Anne longed to mention that of the six Princesses, not one was married, or even engaged to be married. But argument with Lady Catherine on any point was futile.

She could not dance, and knew none of the unmarried men, most of whom were much younger than she, for she was five-and-twenty. There were no offers of marriage. They had waited too long for Mr Darcy.

Then followed a series of unprofitable visits to every country house within reach of a carriage drive. She still remembered with pain the last visit they had made. It had been a long drive, and she had arrived feeling unwell, as she often did, from the motion of the carriage. Her kind hostess had directed the housekeeper to take her upstairs, so that she might lie down. As they were going up the stairs, she heard a flurry of footsteps, a suppressed laugh, and the words, in a girl's voice "Oh dear! Robert, Peter, be quick!" She caught a glimpse of a masculine coattail, just disappearing at the far end of the landing. The young sons and daughter of the house had fled, on hearing the noise of their arrival, and were making their escape down another set of stairs.

A few days later, her mother had announced that they were going to Pemberley, where the new Mrs Darcy was to find a husband for her! Mr and Mrs Darcy, Lady Catherine had explained, owed it to them, after the disgraceful way Anne had been treated, to find her a husband.

"Whom will they find?" she asked. "Who will want to marry me?" she did not like to say "as plain and stupid as I am." Her mother had replied, "Really, Anne, I wish you will not talk such nonsense. Of course you will get a husband. You will have thirty thousand pounds."

So thirty thousand pounds was to be spent. The money would be paid over, and she would never see it. I wish, she thought desperately, they would just give me the money and let me live alone. But of course, the money was not only buying her a husband, it was going to provide a companion for her mother.

Conversation with Lady Catherine was at all times a matter of listening rather than speaking, and the expressions most commonly in use were "Yes, ma'am," and, occasionally, "No, ma'am." Anne was quite used to following her own train of thought in silence. Now she realized that her mother had some time ago ceased speaking. Looking up, she saw that Lady Catherine's face had lost its usual ruddy hue, and was very white. Suddenly Lady Catherine fell forward. Mullins gave a startled exclamation, then, seeing her mistress gasping for breath, screamed. Lady Catherine was in the throes of a sudden, extremely painful sickness. Anne tried to hold her, she twisted and writhed; Anne called to her; she could not reply.

The postilion had felt the movement, even before he heard the noise; he pulled up the horses; the carriage stopped. But even as it did so, Lady Catherine wrenched at the door handle, thrust herself out, and set foot on the step. The carriage jerked to a halt; she slipped; she fell. The ditch at this point was steep and stony; she fell into it, onto the stones.

Mullins cried, "My lady! My lady!" Anne thought she screamed, too; then they were all standing in the road. When Anne, trying to help her mother to stand up, took her arm, Lady Catherine gave a cry of pain, and collapsed back onto the ground. Mullins gasped, "Oh, she is dead!" and went into hysterics. All was fright, distress, and confusion.

Chapter 3

VEHICLES WERE PASSING ON THE ROAD, BUT THE BULK OF THE chaise, and the depth of the ditch, mostly shielded them from view. However, a carriage—a gentleman's carriage by the look of it—did stop, and a sensible-looking woman over the middle age got out, spoke to the coachman, and came toward them. "You are in a sad case," she said. "Can I or my carriage be of use to you?" Anne, frightened, and ashamed of the figure her mother must make, could hardly speak, but managed to stammer out her thanks—"She did not wish to be troublesome, and the carriage had sustained no harm, but they were indeed in difficulty"—and an account of their circumstances.

At this point, Lady Catherine opened her eyes. "Where are we?" she said. "Anne, what are you doing? What is happening? Who is that person? I am very ill," and she lost consciousness again. Mullins screamed "Oh, she is alive!" and stood wringing her hands. Anne and the lady scrambled down into the ditch, and tried to support Lady Catherine, while the coachman and footman maintained that air of lofty indifference which seems to be the attitude of all hired drivers, even though their passengers might happen to be dying.

"Your mother is indeed alive," the lady said, "but we cannot know what ails her. What do you want to do? Would you rather take her to some place where she can get help, though it might hurt her to be moved, or wait here with her and I will see if a doctor can be sent out to you? By the way, my name is Endicott, and I live in Hoddersley."

Anne had never in her life made a decision on behalf of herself, let alone her mother. But there could be but one answer to that. Lady Catherine de Bourgh, Anne knew, would endure any discomfort, any pain, sooner than stay there, sick and distressed, her hair disordered and her clothing soiled, in view of passersby.

"We were on our way to Pemberley," she ventured.

"Pemberley! that is at least fifteen miles from here. I think she is too ill to travel so far."

"Can you tell me, ma'am, where we are?" Anne asked. "Are we close to any town or village?"

"We are within a mile or so of Burley, ahead of us, and four miles the other way from Hoddersley," Mrs Endicott said. "Hoddersley is a big town. You would certainly find everything there that you require."

"We passed through it," Anne said, remembering the noisy town, full of manufactories, with its dirty air and bad smells. "Is Burley the town with the famous medicinal well?"

"Yes," Mrs Endicott said. "Do you know it?"

"I have read about it," Anne said. "Is it not a resort for invalids? Surely, there would be a doctor there? I think perhaps we should go there. Only a mile, and it would be better for my mother. Is that what I should do, ma'am?"

"I cannot make the choice for you or her, my dear; only you can do that," Mrs Endicott said.

Anne took a deep breath. "Then we will go to Burley."

"I think that is the right thing to do. You can be on your way as soon as that silly maid helps your mother into the carriage. The Royal George is the best inn. I will drive there with you, and speak to them. Come, woman! help your mistress. Put your arm round her; that is right. Now, if I lift her on the other side…"

It was done, more quickly than she could have thought possible. Lady Catherine, inert, took up a good deal of space, and Mrs Endicott offered to take Anne in her carriage, but Anne thought she ought to stay with her mother. Mrs Endicott took Mullins up instead, gave directions to the coachman, and bade her a kindly farewell. The door closed, the coachman whipped up his horses, and they were on their way. Anne sat forward awkwardly on the front seat, holding her mother's hand, and trying to tell her calmly that they would soon be there; soon the doctor would make her feel better. Her own mind was in disorder, as she repeated the words, and all she could recall was that the lady had called Mullins—the formidable Mullins—silly.

Twenty years ago, the famous Burley spring was a damp depression in a meadow, where women brought their washing, and the sick sometimes their aching bones. Then progress—or rather the desire for money—arrived. The hot spring, imprisoned in a fine stone casing, was surrounded with a Pump Room, bathhouse, and promenade, and renamed the "Burley Chalybeate." Assembly Rooms, shops, and several hostelries and elegant lodgings sprang up around it. But numerous other springs had been so apotheosed, and many resort towns had hopefully sprung up. The number of visitors to the remote Derbyshire dale was not so great as could be wished. Although the summer was becoming very hot, the hotels were still not full, and the Duchess of Stilbury, whose visit was the most anticipated event of the season, had chosen to hire furnished lodgings rather than stay at the Royal George.

Had it been otherwise, even Mrs Endicott might have had trouble getting any attention for the timid young lady in the close bonnet and old-fashioned dress. As it was, the name of "Lady Catherine de

Bourgh" was all that was needed. The proprietor, the proprietor's wife, the waiters, the chambermaids, the ostlers, the very potboys, all smartened up and bustled themselves about at the prospect of a Lady Catherine; and almost before she knew it, Anne was in possession of a very decent bedchamber, a private sitting-room, and the services of a chambermaid, while in a rather larger bedroom, a capable-looking doctor, hastily summoned, was attending to her mother, with Mullins obeying his every command.

Dr Lawson soon joined her, and told her that Lady Catherine had broken her arm. But her principal problem was a very bad case of poisoning. She had obviously eaten some noxious food, probably some meat that had gone bad in the warm weather. He did not think that her case was desperate, but it was serious; a few hours would show how bad it was. In any case, she must not expect her mother to be well again in a few days, or even weeks. Lady Catherine would require attention by day and night, to a far greater extent than her maid could provide; he would like to send in a sickroom assistant, an excellent woman whom he had employed in several cases; would Miss de Bourgh agree to the expenditure? Anne assented.

"Now, I must leave you," he said. "I have several other cases to see to; but I will return, and Mrs Williams will probably arrive before I do; I will tell them downstairs to send for her as soon as may be, for I think your maid is a little bewildered," and he left.

Anne felt that she, too, was bewildered. But she must rouse herself, she must think. There was money in Lady Catherine's reticule, and she had paid off the post-chaise; but she had engaged herself in a good many expenses. She had no idea of how people arranged to pay for things, when they were from home. Her mother, or her mother's man of business, had always attended to such matters. Things were ordered, and bills paid; Anne had never had more than a few shillings in her own purse. Then, too, they would be expected at Pemberley—but no! her mother had not specified any particular date, no one would be anxious. But she was alone! she, who had never in her life been alone. What was she to do? How was she to go on? All her life, somebody had told her what to do; and now, she must think, she must act for herself.

She thought of writing to Mr Colby, her mother's agent, at Rosings, but the letter must go down into Kent, and then it would certainly take him several days to arrive. The best thing she thought she could do, was to write to Mr and Mrs Darcy, and send the letter by the post; if she had understood her friend of the carriage—Mrs… Mrs Endicott—aright, Pemberley was but fifteen miles distant. Her cousin might be haughty and disdainful, but if she wrote to him, he would certainly assist her. If he did not come himself, he would send someone; maybe his man of business, or the lady who was Georgiana's companion, for Anne did not rate her claims to attention very high. Letters, she had heard, usually arrived on the following day after they were sent. Someone would come, as early as tomorrow—or the next day. Meanwhile, the hotel people, and the doctor, surely would not ask her for any money for a few days—no! of course they would not.

She sat down at the desk, and after a struggle with the bad pen, and the black mud that the hotel called ink, she found the actual composition of the letter very easy; she had something to tell, she had something to ask. She folded the letter and directed it, then looked into her mother's room. No attendant had yet arrived, and Mullins was fully occupied; her mother could not be left alone. The chambermaid had disappeared, and there seemed to be nobody about the hotel who was not frantically busy. In the end, she timidly asked directions of a hurried waiter, and set out, a little nervously, to find the post office.

Chapter 4

THE POST OFFICE WAS LOCATED NOT FAR AWAY, OUTSIDE THE fashionable quarter, but only a couple of streets distant, beside the church, in the old part of the town. It was toward the end of a warm afternoon, the promenade was not busy, and the few strollers took no notice of Anne.

She had never in her life gone beyond the palings of Rosings Park on foot. She had never gone anywhere unaccompanied. She had always been told that her health did not permit her to learn to ride. Her exercise was always limited to a walk in the formal garden, or the grounds, and if she left them, it was for a carriage drive. Usually she drove with her mother, sometimes alone; but "alone," of course, always meant in the company of Mrs Jenkinson. It was quite easy to find her way, but even so, she found the walk to the post office very tiring and trying; she felt that everyone must be staring at her; she wondered what she would do if she were to get lost; and the heat, radiating back from the fronts of the houses, distressed her greatly. The walk, of less than half a mile, seemed dreadfully long. However, she arrived at last; the place was not busy; in fact there were no customers; the civil postmistress took her letter; the letter was sent! It must arrive tomorrow, and her cousins would come and rescue her, or send someone, or write, at least.

The walk back was successfully navigated; but by the time she arrived at the hotel, heat, nervousness, and exhaustion had brought on a bilious head-ache. Her legs were shaking so much that she could scarcely walk up the stairs. She opened the door of her sitting room, to find Dr Lawson seated at the table, writing.

"Ah, my dear young lady," he said. "They told me you were gone out, and I was leaving a note for you. Your mother is no worse, and we certainly need not fear for her life. Her arm has been strapped up, and Mrs Williams is there and knows just what to do for her. But let me look at you! What have you been doing? You are quite white; you are perspiring. The post office? You are knocked up after a walk to the post office? Dear me. Have I one patient, or two? You feel queasy? Yes, I thought so." He strode to the door, and she heard him shouting at the head of the stairs, to someone, to bring a pot of mint tea—"Hot, mind!"—right away. Anne leaned back in a chair, and closed her eyes.

The mint tea made her feel much more comfortable; and she was very soon able to accede to Dr Lawson's request to see any medications that she was in the habit of taking. When he saw the half-dozen bottles, his face changed; he looked very grave, and took them up, one by one, muttering "Yes, very well; but this—no! together with this, my G—, what are they trying to do to the girl? And this—absolutely noxious—absolute poison!" He asked if she had any list of the ingredients used to make them up. "Yes, sir, for the doctor thought, if we were away for a considerable time, I would need more. I think I can find it… yes, here it is."

He looked at it, and said "Miss de Bourgh, may I ask you to do something for me? Will you refrain from taking these medications, for a few days? I think you will find that you do better without them, especially if you will try to spend some time every day in the fresh air. I promise you, that if you feel at all unwell, I will make up something to make you feel better."

"Very well, sir."

"Do you have difficulty eating? Yes, I thought so. It would be surprising if you did not. I will send you some raspberry tea, which I think you will find helpful. It is very simple, very natural, you need fear nothing. We must get you eating a little more, we do not like our young ladies to be quite so thin; we like young ladies a little fatter than this, in Derbyshire. I will tell good Mrs Brown to send you up a very plain supper; you cannot take rich foods, and do not be concerned if you do not feel like eating much, tonight, after the day you have had. But try to drink as much as you can; you may drink water, or lemonade, or tea, but not wine."

"Oh no, sir, I never touch it."

"Now, Miss de Bourgh, I must leave you. You will have but a dull day tomorrow, I am afraid, but you have had a great shock, and would do well to take things easy. You may look in upon your mother, but I have given her something to make her sleep; she will not need any attention from you. Mrs Williams knows just what to do. You can walk round the town as much as you like, the old town or the new, we are very law-abiding people here, no bad characters. Go and drink some of our good spring water, it is very useful, though not such a miracle-worker as some people like to think. And of course you will like to go to church; we are proud of our church, a beautiful old building." And with a courteous farewell he was gone.

Go to church! Good heavens, today was Saturday! Tomorrow was Sunday! She had never given it a thought. Her letter certainly would not be delivered, probably had not yet left the post office. Her cousins would know nothing of her plight until Monday, or more probably Tuesday; and she almost burst into tears, at the thought of her useless, exhausting walk. Well! There was nothing to be done. She must wait. Help would some time come. She lay back and closed her eyes.

The promised supper arrived: some soup, a little roast chicken, and a very good jelly, along with the raspberry tea. Anne found, to her surprise, that she was hungry. The food was simple and good, the portions were small, and best of all, there was no one there to be concerned about what she ate, or how much.

After eating, she wondered whether it really was a good idea to take no medicine at all, whether she should not at least take her opiate; but found that every single bottle was gone. She remembered Dr Lawson working on the catch of his bag, while he was talking; he must have absentmindedly put them in. Never mind! He would certainly bring them back.

She looked in to enquire after her mother. Lady Catherine was asleep, and looked so exhausted, she hardly recognized her. The kind-faced woman who was the sickroom assistant told her not to worry. "I've seen people much worse than her, miss; she will do very well. She will be well enough to be cross tomorrow, you'll see." Anne found herself so tired, nothing really seemed to matter, and although the sun had barely set, she thought she must go to bed. It was refreshing to think that there was nobody who would object, or even care.

But sleep did not come. She had been in the habit of taking laudanum for too long. Anne tossed and turned for some while; then another circumstance arose, to prevent her from sleeping. Her room overlooked the promenade, the hotel was directly opposite the entrance to the Rooms, and it was an assembly night. She heard the horses' hooves, the murmur of people arriving, she heard laughter; in the end she arose, and watched the carriages arrive, the pretty girls and the lively young men. It was a hot night, few wraps were worn; she could see the shimmer of jewels and the glint of embroidery. The music started. Over the laughter and chatter, she could hear it faintly. Soon the street was almost empty, only a few coachmen lingering, a few horses stamping as they stood. She could hear the music clearly now. Anne was still awake when the music stopped and the sound of laughter, the sound of horses' hooves, told her that the dance was over, and the people were going home.

Chapter 5

THE NEXT MORNING WAS CLOSE AND WARM, WITH THE PROMISE of a sultry day. Anne enjoyed the walk to church, for she knew the way, and felt quite safe. The graveyard had a fine view over the surrounding hills and dales, and the old building was, indeed, a beautiful one, though in the old Gothic style. It was pleasant to hear a well-thought-out sermon—very different from poor Mr Collins's miserable efforts—and as she left the building, Dr Lawson greeted her. Crossing the churchyard, she recognized Mrs Endicott, who bowed and smiled, but did not speak. It was enough to send her back to her solitary meal in a cheerful frame of mind.

But the afternoon tried her severely. She had nothing to read, and no one to speak to. Her mother was sleeping most of the time. Awake, she was not, as Mrs Williams had predicted, cross; she was quite unreasonable, and hardly seemed to know where she was. Anne had no recourse but to sit in her room, or to walk again and again around the hot promenade, and look in the windows of the shops. After three or four rounds, she knew their contents by heart: the ugly bonnet with the purple ribbons, the black and yellow boots, the dashing blue shoes, and the pieces of "Derbyshire spar." She knew the titles of—and wished she could read—the books in the window of the bookstore; she knew the pattern of the railings and the very cracks in the pavement.

It was boredom, and not devotion, that induced her to attend the evening service at the church. She felt her motives to be much less than admirable, and what no Christian should entertain: to go to church because she really had nothing else to do! However, when she entered it, the ancient building seemed to welcome her like a friend. It was very different from the church at Rosings, which was a handsome, modern building; but it was a church, it had sheltered others in anxiety and loneliness before her. The monuments on the walls reminded her of her father's memorial; people here, too, had loved, had grieved. She prayed for her mother, and felt reassured.

As she was leaving, an elderly woman, simply dressed but obviously a gentlewoman, came up to her and asked if she was Miss de Bourgh. When she replied that she was, the lady said, "My name is Caldwell. I knew your father. My husband and he were great friends, and I met you when you were a very small child; your parents brought you on a visit to Pemberley."

She enquired after Lady Catherine, and said "My friend Mrs Endicott told me that you were here, and about your situation. I think I should have known you anywhere; you have a great look of your father. We liked him so very much, we were greatly saddened by the news of his death. Now, Miss de Bourgh, what can I do, or what can my husband do, to make things more comfortable for you while you are here?"

Anne did not know what her mother would have thought of this, for Lady Catherine never made any new acquaintance, and always refused to meet new people; but the lady had known her father; it must be proper. And there was one thing she wanted very badly. Hesitantly, she asked if Mrs Caldwell could lend her a book. Any book! or if none were available, a newspaper; she would return it tomorrow, and go to a lending library, but for tonight she had nothing. Poor Anne thought to herself that she would read a cookery book, or a dictionary, if nothing else were to be had.

"If that is all," Mrs Caldwell said, "we shall be delighted; my husband has a large library, and I am very fond of reading myself. Our home is quite close by, and you may come and choose for yourself. But Mrs Endicott is staying with us, and I do not know if you and your mother would wish for her acquaintance. The Endicotts are not people of rank; her husband is a publisher and bookseller. If you prefer, tell me what you like, and my maid shall bring a few books to the hotel, so that you may choose something."

"Distinctions of rank are thought to matter greatly," Anne replied, "but Mrs Endicott was kind, and that matters more. My father told me he read a book by a French writer who said that savages are more noble than we are, because they do not care about such things. That is, I tried to read it; I think that is what it said. In any case, I would be happy to make Mrs Endicott's acquaintance."

"My dear, that is just the kind of thing your father would have said."

The Caldwells lived in a respectable-looking stone house, on one of the streets near the church. Anne found herself in a spacious apartment, its walls crowded with books, looking out onto an enclosed garden. In it, Mrs Endicott was sitting with two men, shaded from the last rays of the sun by a big copper-beech tree. Mrs Caldwell called them in, and introduced her husband and her son. Mr Edmund Caldwell was a stocky, youngish man, not handsome, but with kind, bright eyes.

"I remember your father well," the elder Mr Caldwell told her. "He was passionately interested in stones—he loved the fossils in our hills—and we wrote a great many letters to each other." Anne was looking at several very big fossils, skillfully mounted, standing on tables and shelves. "I think there are some specimens like these in the library at Rosings," she ventured, "there are several cabinets of smaller ones, too, and many of them have the word 'Derbyshire' on the labels."

"We collected them together," Mr Caldwell said. "We had some wonderful days in the hills. You came with us, Edmund; and young Fitzwilliam Darcy. I can see him now, scrabbling about with his hammer, so serious. He looked up to you, Edmund, then, for he was only eight years old, and you were ten; and that handsome little fellow, George Wickham, came along, but he did nothing, just ran about, he never would apply himself. You were only three, Miss de Bourgh, but your nurse walked you out to meet us, a little toddling thing in a pink dress."

His wife said. "I remember it well. She wanted to do everything that the others did, and picked up a pebble from the roadside, and brought it to you, saying 'Look, Mr Caldwell, this is a beauty!'" She smiled at Anne.

"All stones are beautiful," said Mr Edmund Caldwell. "Yes, they are; even those by the roadside. They have colours in them, they have gleams, they have traces of the fire wherein they were made. They will shine, if you cut and polish them.

"Look, Miss de Bourgh," and he picked up a small platter made of blue stone. "Look, see the patterns in this, see the swirls of colour. This is the blue john, our own Derbyshire stone. It is found nowhere else in the world. It is fragile; it will smash easily. But how beautiful it is!" and he smiled at her.

"It is indeed," Anne said, and smiled back at him, holding the little dish in her hand.

"We have a property up in the hills," Mr Caldwell said. "The soil is too thin to do much farming, and my son had the idea of developing a lead mine, which is doing very well."

"Yes, the lead mine is doing well," Mrs Endicott said, "but are you making anything from the little blue john mine?"

"Well, it makes no money," said Edmund Caldwell, "but I believe beautiful things can be made from this stone, if we can but learn to work it. It is an amusement—or should I say, a passion?"

"Now Miss de Bourgh, you must choose a book," Mrs Caldwell said. "Would you like a novel, or something more serious? Miss de Bourgh has been reading the French authors," she told the others.

"I did, a little, but I find reading French very hard, too hard for pleasure."

"And their terrible ideas," said Mrs Endicott.

"No," said Edmund Caldwell. "They have wonderful ideas, about liberty and equality."

"But look at the dreadful things they have done. Such wicked people. Their ideas must be wrong."

"But, excuse me," Anne said. "Are we right to condemn the ideas, because some of the people did wicked things? We all know what it is to have good principles, but not do such good things as we know we ought."

"One idea they have, which I support with all my heart," said Edmund Caldwell, "and that is, liberty. Slavery is wrong, tyranny is wrong. Nobody should be allowed to tyrannise over any other human being."

"But is it right, to protest it by violent means?" asked Mrs Endicott.

"Come, come," said Mrs Caldwell, "Miss de Bourgh came here for something to read, not an argument. We argue all the time, Miss de Bourgh, in this house. There is only one provision: that nobody is allowed to get angry. Now, Miss de Bourgh, would you like a novel?"

"I am not in the habit of novel reading. My mother does not approve of them, and there are very few in our house." As she spoke, she was looking along the shelves, and took down a volume: *An Enquiry into the Original State and Formation of the Earth* by John Whitehurst. "I have read this; it is in my father's library."

"I know it," said Mr Edmund Caldwell. "It was not published recently, but it is very good, and there is a great deal in it about our county."

"Do you know," said Mrs Endicott, "that in a short while a great map will be published, of all the British Isles, showing the rocks that lie underneath, in every place? And he will buy it, will you not, Edmund?"

"Yes, indeed," he said. "Whatever the cost, I shall buy it."

"Come, try a novel," Mrs Caldwell said, smiling at Anne. "Do try. There can be no harm. You want something a little lighter to read before you go to sleep."

"If you give her the last one you lent to me, she will not sleep at all," said Mrs Endicott. "She wants no *Horrid Mysteries,* or midnight frighteners."

"No, no," said Mrs Caldwell. "I have one here that is very pretty, and harmless. Now, where is it? On this table here, I think, for I put it down the other day…"

While she hunted for it, Anne looked further along the shelves, and found a small pamphlet: *An Account of some Curious Derbyshire Rock Formations* by Edmund Caldwell. Publisher: John Endicott.

"Oh!" she said. "Did you write this, sir? I would dearly like to read it."

"You may keep it, Miss de Bourgh," said its author. "We have a good number of unsold copies."

"Oh, come," said Mrs Endicott. "It did not sell at all badly."

"No, but we can certainly spare one for Miss de Bourgh."

Meanwhile, the elder Mr Caldwell had been looking through an untidy writing desk. He now came toward them, with an envelope in his hand.

"This is something that you may like to see, my dear," he said, sliding out a letter, and holding it out to her.

The paper was not new. Anne saw the address *My dear Caldwell, I was so pleased to receive your letter,"* She saw the first words *"My dear Caldwell, I was so pleased to receive your letter,"* and knew her father's hand. She could see him, sitting at the desk in his library, writing, while she sat close by in a big armchair, playing with her doll. She felt the tears rising to her eyes, she felt her face convulse; she began to cry, and found that she could not stop.

Chapter 6

A YOUNG LADY WHO FAINTS MAY AWAKE CHIVALROUS SENTIMENTS in gentlemen; a young lady who weeps engenders only a strong desire to be elsewhere. By the time Anne was recovered enough to look up, both Mr Caldwells had disappeared. Mrs Endicott was holding her hand, Mrs Caldwell was proffering a clean handkerchief, and a maid was bringing in a tea-tray.

"Oh, what must you think of me?" was her first exclamation.

"We think that you have had a dreadful two days, and are tired and distressed," was Mrs Caldwell's reply. "Now, Miss de Bourgh, here is a cup of tea; do you drink it, and then you shall wash your face and feel better."

The tea did make Anne feel better, and then she found that Mrs Endicott's carriage had been ordered to take her back to the hotel. In spite of her protests, she was glad of it. When they got outside they found that it was needed, for the sultry weather of the past few days had broken, and a heavy rain had begun. Both ladies went with her, bringing a number of novels; and saw to putting her to bed, and the ordering of a bowl of bread and milk. She felt much more comfortable, but her mind was still in great distress.

"Mr Caldwell, oh, poor Mr Caldwell. What a terrible thing for me to do. I must have made him feel so dreadful," she lamented.

"He is only sad for you," said Mrs Caldwell, who knew that her husband was, in fact, saddened and distressed beyond measure. Anne knew it, too. Tired as she was, and late as it was, she must not allow her friends to leave, without at least trying to put the matter right. An idea came to her.

"Do you think," she asked, "that Mr Caldwell would allow me to keep the letter? It chances that, since I was always at home, my father never wrote me a letter. I have nothing in his writing, which is why I was so overcome. It would mean a great deal to me, to have it."

"My dear!" exclaimed Mrs Caldwell joyfully, "it will make him so happy. I can answer for it—he will be delighted."

The two ladies left, promising to call the next day and take her for a walk to see the beauties of the surrounding countryside. Anne lay back and closed her eyes. What a pleasant thing it was, to be with people who talked about books, and ideas; and who argued but never got angry! She remembered Edmund Caldwell, smiling at her over the little stone platter; the thought came into her mind that Mr Edmund Caldwell had smiled at her very agreeably indeed.

She found, it seemed only a few minutes later, that she had slept the night through.

Monday dawned with some improvement to Lady Catherine. Her assistants assured Anne that she would sleep a great deal, and was best not disturbed, for the time being.

The rain had stopped, but the roads were still wet. Mr and Mrs Caldwell arrived, and told her that Mr Edmund had returned to his home to attend to his business. "He spends a great deal of time with us," said his mother, "and I think the reason is, that he has never married. He says that he has never seen the woman he wants to marry, and that the lead mine, and the quarry, must come first with him, and I suppose it is very right that they should; but I should like to see him with a good, kind wife, and some little children of his own."

Mr Caldwell, smiling affectionately, handed over to Anne her father's letter. She thanked him again and again, and put it away, as a treasure to be kept for life. "I would not deny myself the pleasure of waiting on you, my dear," he said, "but I do not propose to stay; the weather is not suitable for a walk, all the field ways will be swamped, and the ladies have had the idea of taking you into the warm bath."

Anne felt doubtful.

"There are only ladies there during the morning hours. It is very harmless, and very pleasant," said Mrs Endicott.

"And health-giving," added Mrs Caldwell. "I am sure good Dr Lawson will approve, for he always recommends it. Come, Miss de Bourgh, you will enjoy it, I am sure; and if you do not like it, we will undertake to bring you straight back, at any moment you choose."

The bathhouse was large, cavernous, and rather ill-lit. It seemed very strange, to be in such a place, and then to be so strangely dressed, but the smiles of the other ladies reassured her—and indeed, they did all cut such comic figures! It was impossible not to be amused, and they all started laughing together. She entered the water timorously, Mrs Caldwell holding her hand, but was at once conscious of the extraordinary warmth, and the feeling both of comfort to her limbs and reassurance to her mind. She began gently moving about, enjoying the sensation of the water flowing about her. "How wonderful it is!" she whispered.

"And how strange to think," said Mrs Caldwell, "that this flow of warmth, of comfortable, gentle warmth, comes from those terrible fires deep within the earth!"

Her enjoyment was such that she kept asking for a little more time, and they actually had to insist on her coming out at last. She thought it was a long time since she had felt so well.

The sense of well-being stayed with her throughout the day.

Lady Catherine awoke toward the end of the afternoon. Her attendants were pleased with her progress; sitting up in bed in her lace wrapper, she was fully able to converse. She was, as Mrs Williams had predicted, well enough to be cross; and she availed herself of the fact to be very cross indeed. Anne had to relate the history of the previous evening and of the morning—or as much of it as she thought her mother needed to hear. She said nothing of her tears, or the letter, only that the Caldwells had taken her home to borrow a book, and taken her into the bath.

Lady Catherine was not pleased. "Caldwell? Caldwell? Who are these people? I have no recollection of ever meeting anybody of that name. Sir Lewis was in the habit of making odd friends; but that does not mean that his wife and daughter are obliged to know them. We may have been acquainted, very slightly, but twenty years ago—you are talking about twenty years ago. I certainly have no recollection of any letter of condolence from them, when Sir Lewis died. These people are probably trying to use your situation to claim a connection. Here you are alone in the place and unprotected, and they want to profit from it. As for Mrs Endicott, I recollect *her* perfectly, and am quite sure that that was what she was doing: she is certainly one of those people who will do anything to get acquainted with a person of rank. You are to have nothing more to do with them, Anne."

Anything more unjust, Anne could not imagine!

What was she to do? Never, in her life, had she disobeyed her mother; always, her mother had decided what was right and what should be done.

Suddenly, she recalled Mr Edmund Caldwell's remark: "Nobody should tyrannise over another person." What would *he* think, if he saw her putting up with injustice to his parents, only because she was afraid?

Taking a deep breath, and in rather a tremulous voice, she said, "As far as you are concerned, ma'am, you are free to reject the acquaintance; but I am not. These people have been kind to me, and I do not believe they did it from any idea of advantage or flattery—they are not in the least like poor Mr Collins. But I have accepted their friendship, I have indebted myself to them, and it would be wrong—it would be unjust—to turn my back on them now."

She waited for the sky to fall in.

But to her surprise, her mother only said, "Well, well; but I will have nothing to do with it. I will not receive them."

"Very well, ma'am."

As for Anne's letter to Pemberley, it was quite unnecessary, she said; *she* would have written in due course. There was no need of money; she had banknotes and a letter of credit in her jewel-case.

One thing, and one thing only, had pleased Lady Catherine: the Master of Ceremonies had called, and though of course she had not been able to receive him, he had left compliments, and the promise of any assistance she might require—any assistance! Anything!—and the library subscription list, together with the list of those who had attended Saturday's assembly.

She was reading both with interest: "Lady Southwell, the Honourable Henry and Mrs Willington, Doctor and Mrs Rigsby,

Captain Stephens, the Reverend Marcus Appleby… That is very well for so small a place, and the season hardly begun; and they tell me the Duchess of Stilbury is expected almost any day, with her brother, Lord Francis Meaburn. You might do very well here, Anne, if you will but pay attention to a more proper kind of people."

The next few days continued in the same pattern; her friends took her to the baths each morning, and in the afternoon they walked. The country around was magnificent, and Anne found she gained strength every day. Still there was no response from the Darcys, and Lady Catherine decided that Anne's letter had gone astray, otherwise they never would have neglected her. Clearly, it was Anne's fault; Anne had written the direction too ill. But it did not matter, she did not need them.

On Thursday, Anne returned to the hotel toward the end of the morning. She entered her sitting room, and found two people there. One was her cousin Darcy; the other, a young lady, tall and handsome. It must be Mrs Darcy—but surely the lady she remembered did not look like this? Surely Miss Elizabeth Bennet was smaller, livelier-looking, and had not such dark hair?

The lady crossed the room, took both Anne's hands in hers, and cried, "You are my cousin, Anne. Oh, poor Anne, what an unpleasant time you have had! We are so sorry!"

It was her cousin, Georgiana Darcy.

Chapter 7

DARCY'S GREETING TO HIS COUSIN WAS AS AFFECTIONATE AS Georgiana's. He expressed over and over their concern, their desire to support and comfort her, and their regret that she had been left for so many days, unassisted by them. His manner to her was that of a kind and affectionate brother, rather than the distant, haughty cousin she had always known. Marriage, she thought, had wrought a great improvement in him.

Anne's letter had, by exceptional activity on the part of the post office—that is, a nephew of the postmistress having a sweetheart in service at Pemberley—actually been delivered to the house on the Saturday evening. But it was addressed to "Mr Darcy," and he was away from home on business. His steward, recognising the name "de Bourgh," had paid the postage, but pretty well knew that his master would be in no especial hurry to get a letter from that particular sender. The significance of the initial "A" instead of "C de Bourgh" had escaped his notice. The letter lay on Darcy's desk until he returned, late on Wednesday.

"And nobody looked at it," Georgina said. "His man of business saw it, but seeing it was a private letter, he did not open it. Oh, Anne, to think of your letter lying there, and you alone here, and wretched!" It was clear that Georgiana's tender heart was wrung. Anne felt, in her own mind, that it was a quite providential occurrence, for she had *not* been wretched, at least beyond the distress of the first day or so. She had enjoyed herself, and more to the point, she had thought and acted for herself for the first time in her life. Her time in Burley had done her a great deal of good. But they had got her in their minds as an ill-used heroine. It might be ill-natured, and would certainly be difficult, to disabuse them. In any case, it was causing them to treat her with very affectionate solicitude, which it would surely be ungracious to refuse.

"The letter was discovered so late in the day," Darcy said, "that we could not set out, and we decided to leave very early this morning."

He and his sister had come to Burley with the intention of staying, if necessary; of hiring a house, if it were thought advisable; of bringing them both to Pemberley, if it could be done; in short, of doing anything and everything that might be of use or comfort.

But Lady Catherine refused to be moved. The doctor had assured Mr Darcy that her arm was well strapped up, and that she would feel little discomfort from the jolting of a well-sprung carriage. She thought otherwise; she was sure that it would hurt her a great deal. The truth was, Lady Catherine was not at all anxious to get to Pemberley, where the former Miss Elizabeth Bennet was mistress. She was extremely comfortable in the hotel, where her presence was highly valued. She was being very well looked after, and her slightest wish was obsequiously carried out. And the Duchess was arriving in a day or so: "I should like to meet her. I would be pleased to make her acquaintance, for the family is a connection of ours. And, Darcy, my carriage will be arriving at Pemberley sometime; see to it, will you?"

Anne might go with them, she said; it would be well to remove Anne from Burley, where she had been associating with the scaff and raff of the place. Mr Darcy had tried in vain to make her understand that the Caldwells were old acquaintances, and that Edmund Caldwell was a friend of his childhood. "I even explained to her that Mrs Caldwell is a second cousin, by marriage, of Lady Louisa Benton," he said. "But she would have none of it; she said she had heard that their son was a stonemason, or a quarryman, or some such thing. Nothing will convince her that he is one of the most respected men in the country, and a very good fellow. Never mind, cousin, we will get them to Pemberley, and you shall meet them again. His home is little more than five miles from us. He and I will have some good talks, too. Nobody is so good a talker as Edmund Caldwell!"

Whether all of Mr Darcy's present good temper derived from his happiness in marriage, or whether some of it was due to the fact that he was not going to have to act as host to Lady Catherine in the near future, it would perhaps be as well not to enquire. At all events, he was in a fine flow of spirits, ready to do anything that would promote his cousin's comfort, and anxious to get her to Pemberley as soon as might be.

To Anne's great satisfaction, Darcy and Georgiana insisted, before they would quit Burley, on calling on Mr and Mrs Caldwell to thank them for their kindness to her, and to engage them to spend a few days at Pemberley. The promise was willingly given; they would come, as soon as their son should be able to be of the party.

By late afternoon, Anne was sitting in an open carriage, admiring the magnificent countryside, on the way to Pemberley. In an open carriage, she had no tendency to biliousness, and felt, indeed, as well as she had ever been. It was a clear, windy day, the shadows of the clouds chased each other across the hillsides, and the fields and trees were resplendent in their summer green. On every side of her was beauty; as she gazed around, she could not keep from smiling, and her eyes were bright with pleasure. No one would have recognised her as the forlorn little figure who had wept her heart out on the Caldwells' sofa a few days before.

Mrs Darcy had sent her love, they told her, and had wanted to come, but she was expecting shortly to be confined, and they had felt that the fifteen-mile journey was too much for her to undertake. "What my brother means is," said Georgiana, "that she is so precious to him, he would not dream of letting her do it, though she wanted to. He put on his *black* look, and she had to stay. She has had to be content with getting the prettiest possible room ready for you. But we thought a lady should come, so I accompanied him. Mrs Annesley is with her, of course, and Colonel Fitzwilliam is there, too. He is always so kind." How pretty she looks, Anne thought; the fresh air has turned her complexion pink.

"Is Colonel Fitzwilliam staying with you?" Anne asked. "We heard that his regiment was sent overseas, and that he was dreadfully injured in action."

"Yes, he is here," said Darcy. "A bullet grazed his face, and he is somewhat disfigured; and another lodged in his shoulder—he has some trouble using his right arm. But the doctors are pleased with his progress; he will be well again in time."

"Oh, how terrible!"

"Do not say so to him," Darcy said. "He makes nothing of it; he will only say that appearances do not matter to a soldier. All he wants to do is to rejoin his comrades."

"He was mentioned in the dispatches," Georgiana said. "His regiment is very proud of him. Look, Anne, there is Pemberley;

there, you see, through the trees and across the water. This is one of my favourite views."

"It should be," said Darcy, smiling. "She has drawn and painted it twenty times at least."

He began rallying his sister, teasing her that whenever she could not get the drawing right, she put in a tree branch; she was laughing. Anne looked at the sunlit reaches of the park, and the house in its splendid setting. She had lived in an imposing house all her life, and the size and magnificence of Pemberley did not impress her. But Rosings stood on level ground, with no views beyond its formal gardens. Here was an open prospect, the dappled light and shade, the fine trees, the stream, all leading the eye out to glorious views over hill and valley. She thought, "This is what my mother intended for me, that I should be mistress of this." To be mistress of Pemberley would indeed be something!

But none of its wealth and grandeur, she could see, was of any value to the owner of Pemberley, compared with the beautiful young woman who stood waiting on the terrace, in all the bloom of expectant motherhood. He leaped out of the carriage toward her; she ran to him. There was that lighting glance that she had seen between them at Rosings; but now it was more: it was a look of perfect happiness, perfect delight! After a few words with her husband, Elizabeth Darcy came toward her, and greeted her with a kind smile and handclasp. It was no wonder, she thought, that her cousin was a different man; marriage with Elizabeth would make any man happy. Suddenly the thought darted through her: more than anything in the world, I would like to make someone as happy as that.

Chapter 8

"WELL, MRS DARCY," SAID HER HUSBAND, AS SOON AS THEY were alone together, "what do you think now?"

"I shall never forget the sense of relief, as the carriage came into view. I saw only two ladies in it; one was Georgiana and the other was clearly *not* Lady Catherine," Elizabeth said. "We have been spared! But I was never so surprised in my life as when I saw your cousin Anne! She is just as thin and small as ever, but she holds herself better; she looks so much livelier, and she smiles and talks much more readily."

"I never realised before how much she resembles her father," said Darcy. "I am sorry you did not know him; I was very fond of him. Dr Lawson asked to speak to me, before she arrived at the hotel this morning. He believes that this poor health of hers is due to nothing more than bad medicine and lack of food. He told me she has been taking a mixture of substances that would damage the constitution of the healthiest person; they have depressed her appetite and harmed her nerves, and she has been eating far too little. I never did like that doctor my aunt employs; I believe his only concern was to flatter her, and feather his own nest by prescribing more and more rubbish, for which, of course, she pays him. And since he declared that Anne was ill, ill she had to be."

"The poor girl! It is monstrous!" exclaimed Elizabeth indignantly.

"No," said Darcy, musingly, "my aunt is not a monster. She means no harm. She is a capable and clever woman. Rosings is as well managed as Pemberley, and her tenants speak of her with respect, though not with affection. She would never, for example, tell a lie, or swindle one of her tenants. She has two serious faults: one is that she has far too much regard for rank. The other is that, whatever is going forward, whatever is needed to be done, she must be the one to do it; the one to plan, to arrange, to carry out. She cannot allow anyone else to control anything. Her man of business must always consult with her first, and do exactly as she sees fit; she leaves nothing to his judgment. Did you know that the Rosings property is not entailed? Sir Lewis made a will soon after they were married, leaving everything to her, house, land, and money; for he said that he knew she would look after it well, and that where there is an entail, the eldest son always becomes expensive, and selfish."

"Yes, because he cannot be disinherited. It is a great pity that they had only one child, and that a daughter. She would have managed any number of noisy, self-willed sons."

"She reminds me sometimes," Darcy said, "of Queen Elizabeth. I am sure that, if she were in charge of the parliament, the country would be well governed."

"I seem to recall," said Elizabeth, "that Queen Elizabeth took almost twenty years to think whether she would cut off the head of the poor Queen of Scots. If Lady Catherine had to decide, I do not think that she would take twenty minutes. But now, what about Anne? It seems to me that now she is here, and without her mother, we have a heaven-sent chance to do some good. I should like to, for I feel she has had but a poor life of it, at Rosings."

"I believe that my aunt is, in a sense, right; we owe Anne something—or at least, I do. Because of me, she has been allowed to spend years in the vain expectation that we would marry."

"Could you not have made it clear that you did not intend to marry her?"

"You may well ask, but though clearly it was, for Lady Catherine, a thing understood, it was never referred to, or not plainly. I was frequently asked to Rosings, but there was always a reason: Fitzwilliam was coming to stay, or the pheasants needed shooting, or my advice was wanted about some matter on the estate. There was never a moment when I might stand up and say, 'Madam, I am not going to marry your daughter.' It is not an easy thing to do."

"I think," Elizabeth said, "that we must do precisely what your aunt has asked us to do; we must find a husband for her."

"It will not be as easy as my aunt thinks; her portion is very large, but she is five-and-twenty, and although her looks have improved, I would not call her handsome. I would not wish her to marry a man who only wanted her for the sake of her money."

"Do you think," said Elizabeth, hesitantly, "that she and your cousin Fitzwilliam might like to marry?"

"Fitzwilliam? He has known her for years, and I have never seen anything of affection—anything beyond cousinly regard."

"Well," said his wife, "I think they would be very well suited. They are close in age, equal in rank, and they know each other. Her money would be in good hands, and it would be very useful to him."

"But he is a soldier, and he loves the life. If she married him, she must go where he goes, and follow the drum. Would her health be adequate for such an existence?"

"Well, there is another matter that I think I should mention to you. My dear, has it occurred to you that Georgiana is becoming very fond of him?"

Darcy looked astounded. "I think it is only a schoolgirl's admiration," Elizabeth said, "but it might become more."

"Fitzwilliam is as good a man as ever lived—but he is too old for her."

"I believe," said Elizabeth, "that your cousin's wounds, and his courage, have had a great effect on her. There is a sort of chivalry in Georgiana. I think that she fell in love with Wickham, you know, because he represented himself as ill-used, neglected, and lonely. I talked with Colonel Fitzwilliam a little today—no! of course I did not mention my suspicions—but I am pretty sure that there is nothing on his side beyond the natural affection of a man for a younger cousin. He is a man of honour, and would never try to gain a young girl's affection for the sake of money. But it might make Georgiana unhappy."

"Good heavens! What can I do? This place is his home, until he is fit to rejoin his regiment. I cannot send him away."

"No, you cannot. The best we can do is to make sure that she has other choices, other interests. We have lived here, you know, very happily since we married, and, my love, I would wish for nothing more—but our comfortable, elegant family circle is very restricted. I believe that, for Georgiana, there should be a more varied society. In the ordinary way, she would have had a season in London, but as things are, we cannot give her that. Let us see how many things we can do to provide her with other people who she might admire or love. It could not be other than good for Anne, too."

"We must go to the assemblies," her husband said, "in Lambton and Burley. We have neighbours whom we can invite for dinner parties, and musical evenings. We can do much more than we have done. Summer is coming, there are race meetings, there are even cricket matches. I would see Anne more occupied, too—stay!—suppose we engage Georgiana, as an affectionate cousin, to help us with Anne? Would not that chivalry of hers be well engaged—to give Anne new interests and occupations—to look after her health— even to look for a husband for her?"

"Yes, indeed it would; it is the very thing. I will talk to her tomorrow."

The morrow, for Anne, brought surprises indeed. She and her cousin Georgiana had a delightful drive around the park in Mrs Darcy's pony carriage. In the course of it, it transpired that Georgiana had an inordinate number of dresses, outgrown or outmoded, that only needed a little cutting down, and a few stitches, for Anne to be able to wear them. "And Anne dear, the Caldwells are coming soon, maybe next week. You must have something fashionable to wear!"

Anne was a little doubtful. What would her mother think of her wearing such thin, fashionable muslin gowns—she would call them flimsy and unseemly—as Georgiana was wearing?

"Oh, but everyone wears them," said Georgiana firmly. "Do but try, let us go back to the house and try. It would oblige me so much, for I made several foolish purchases in London, and I have a green sprig muslin that does not suit me at all, and a dark blue silk, and I know that they would look pretty on you, and I would not feel so badly about having spent my brother's money; not that he cares, for he would buy me anything that I wanted. And you know, Anne, your mother need never know!" They did indeed look very pretty, even with the hems trailing past her ankles, and onto the floor, and the sewing maid promised to alter them as rapidly as might be.

Then Mrs Darcy's maid, who, it seemed, had very little to do, got at her hair, and created a new, very becoming style for her. Mrs Annesley offered to teach her to play the piano. Her cousin Darcy gave her the freedom of his library. And Colonel Fitzwilliam, quite unprompted, pointed out that Mrs Darcy could not, in her present circumstances, exercise her mare—such a gentle creature!—and offered to teach Anne to ride, thus raising Mrs Darcy's hopes quite considerably.

Chapter 9

THE MAKING OVER OF GEORGIANA'S CLOTHES, FOR SUCH A SMALL lady as Anne, proved quite difficult, for Georgiana was sturdy as well as tall. However, Mrs Reynolds, the Pemberley housekeeper, got to hear of the matter. She had loved Lady Anne Darcy, who had always been very well dressed, and thought it a great pity that her niece should be wearing unfashionable clothes that did not become her at all; the Pemberley ladies should be elegant! She produced several lengths of silk and muslin, bought at one time or another but never used. If Miss did not object to quite a simple style, she said, a couple of day dresses and an evening gown could be very quickly made up. And as for the style—yes! maybe in France, where they did nasty things, the ladies wore them with so little underneath that the unseemly creatures must surely catch their death, but Miss would see how comfortable such dresses were, and quite proper, with a nice thick English petticoat underneath!

The dresses were ready before the Caldwells arrived. Anne was delighted with them; they suited her well, and with her newly styled hair, she was able to play her part in the initial dinner party with a confidence she had seldom felt before. Visitors came to Pemberley almost every day, and many had been very agreeable, but to see *them* again was so comfortable! She could talk with parents and son alike, with as much ease as if they were old acquaintances. Mr and Mrs Caldwell treated her like a daughter, and it was amazing how many of the same books she and Edmund liked!

The first evening, as they were all sitting together after dinner, Georgiana suddenly said, "Do you know, brother, that Anne says she cannot dance?"

"Not dance? Why, how is this?"

Anne admitted that she had, of course, been taught to dance, but being out of practice, unwell, and shy, she had not been able to the last time she was at a ball.

"That will not do at all," said Mrs Darcy. "We are going to the Lambton assembly quite soon. What can be done?"

"If you would like, Madam," said Mrs Annesley, "I would be very happy to play the piano, and we could walk Miss de Bourgh through a few figures, at any time."

"Oh!" cried Georgiana, "let us dance now! We could make up, let me see... we are one... three... five women, and four men. We can make up three couples, if Mrs Annesley will play for us, and Anne can watch."

"I have a better idea," said Elizabeth. "I will play, you can make up four couples, and Anne can join in," and she sat down at the pianoforte, and began a country dance.

It was strange, but after one walk through, Anne had no trouble at all in picking up the figures! Among friends, in whom she had confidence, her shyness vanished. She turned, and cast, and set, and curtseyed, and yet had leisure to notice that Colonel Fitzwilliam was by far the best dancer, and Edmund Caldwell the worst.

After this, they danced every evening. There were walks every day in the park, but soon everyone became ambitious, and a walk to the celebrated fossil face was proposed.

"How far is it?" Anne asked.

"I think it cannot be more than two miles," her cousin Darcy said.

"A little more, I believe," said Mr Caldwell. "Edmund, the fossil rock face—is it not about two miles distant from here?"

"I think so," his son said. "It is a while since I walked it, and then it was from my own home; but I think it cannot be much more."

"Two miles! Oh, that is nothing," said Georgiana.

"Yes, but wait a moment," her brother said. "It is not a ride, remember, you were talking of a walk."

"Yes, but two miles, we walk almost that far when we go into the village."

"But that is there and back."

"Oh! I had forgot, we must come back."

"Yes, but you will be coming downhill," said Mr Caldwell. "There is quite a steep uphill slope to get to the face."

"It is all very well for most of you," Mrs Darcy said, "but I confess that I have not, at this moment, such a burning interest in rock faces, as would lead me to walk four miles, in total, for the reward of seeing one. I think that I will be quite happy to stay at home."

"And I will stay, and keep an eye on you," Darcy said, "for I have some business matters that cannot well be put off. My steward has been looking at me reproachfully for several days now."

Mr and Mrs Caldwell, however, were not to be held back, and constituted themselves the party's guides and principal mentors. "Indeed, my mother knows far more than I do," Edmund Caldwell said. "And my husband knows more," Mrs Caldwell said, "than both of us together."

"I know very little of such matters," said Colonel Fitzwilliam, "and my lack of knowledge embarrasses me; but if you will have me along, I will promise to be an attentive, if not an apt, pupil."

Since arriving at Pemberley, Anne had gained a good deal of strength, but walking still fatigued her, and she much preferred to ride. Colonel Fitzwilliam was very pleased with her progress, and she delighted in her morning rides, which allowed her to see a great deal of the beauty of the park. She did not like to say that she was not up to a walk of four miles, but clearly, Colonel Fitzwilliam did not intend to go on horseback: suppose she started out, and could not complete the distance? Would she not be better advised to stay at home? Or would she be able to ride? Perhaps Georgiana or a groom would come with her? These thoughts had scarcely begun to occupy her mind, when Mrs Annesley proposed a plan. "That is too much of a distance for me," she said, "but is the road fit for the pony carriage?"

"Perfectly," Darcy said, "as long as the weather is fine. It is a pleasant country lane, except for the last few hundred yards, when you must leave the path, which is but a track by that time, and walk—or rather scramble—up to the face. We did it easily when we were boys, and even now it would not be too difficult for anyone wearing good stout shoes."

"If I were to drive the little carriage," said Mrs Annesley, "it could be useful to bring something to drink, and perhaps some sandwiches, for I think—am I not right?—that the countryside is quite remote, and there are no villages, no inns or taverns. And if any of the ladies are afraid of fatigue, one of them could take a seat with me, at any time, or ride with me for the whole of the way." Anne immediately closed with the offer, and it was agreed that they should go together.

Chapter 10

THE DAY DAWNED FINE, WITH A GENTLE BREEZE. ANNE'S enjoyment was assured from the start by the knowledge that she was looking her best. It was Georgiana who had remarked that Anne never looked well in a bonnet. Neither close-brim, wide-brim, nor poke suited her small, delicate features; she merely looked "as prim as a governess," said Georgiana. She had insisted on Anne trying on all her hats, and on giving her several. The one she was wearing today had been agreed by all to be the prettiest, with its wide, shady brim and green ribbons, and went very well with her new cambric gown.

So attired, she enjoyed the ride with Mrs Annesley, and a comfortable discussion of the evening gown she was to wear at the Lambton assembly. It was not too long before they came to the point where the carriage must be abandoned. Ahead of them they saw the rest of the party, who had begun to walk up a grassy path, to the actual face, and who kindly stopped to allow them to catch up. The ascent to begin with was not steep, and, everyone encouraging everyone else, was comfortably achieved. Soon their destination was before them, a steep, grayish line of rock, with the ground beneath it strewn with gray chippings and bits of stone. Here there was a short climb to a sort of rock shelf.

"I am afraid," said Mr Caldwell, "that the best specimens have been taken out long ago. It is about twenty years since we were here, and many other enthusiasts have been here since then. But one never knows, there may be even better things still hidden."

Georgiana was particularly interested, and getting up to quite a high point, soon called to Mr Caldwell, "Oh, sir! Do come! I am sure there is something very strange here! Do but look! These rounded shapes, these kind of stripes, are they not shells, or animals?"

"It may well be," he replied, "but I cannot get up there to see; I am afraid I am not as young as I was. Here, Colonel Fitzwilliam, do you take my hammer, and get up there with her." The Colonel obeyed, but the ledge where Georgiana stood was not large enough to hold them both, and she yielded up her place and started on the way down again.

"Dear me," said Mr Caldwell. "I remember Darcy, scrambling up to that very ledge, and young Wickham, making his way up beside him, and saying 'Get out, Darcy, do, you have been up there long enough, get out, and let me try what I can do.' You must remember him well, Miss Darcy, for I know you always liked one another. I hear he is married. I hear he is to come back to the neighbourhood very soon—"

"No," said Mrs Caldwell, "you are mistaken, my dear. It is young Mr Wicking, the churchwarden's son…" but as they were speaking, Georgiana, who had been carefully making her way down, suddenly seemed to twist herself away, and apparently misjudged her footing, for she slipped and fell.

There was a general outcry, and everyone ran to assist her. She had not fallen far, but she had fallen awkwardly, and appeared unable to rise. As Anne, who was nearest, got to her, she saw that Georgiana was crying, with heavy, gasping sobs.

"Oh, how bad is it?" Anne cried, and put her arms round her. Georgiana did not reply.

Mrs Annesley, coming up, said, "Come, Georgiana, come, my dear, let me see. Where does it hurt?" But Georgiana only cried out, and gasped. Mrs Annesley asked, "Does that hurt? Does that?" as she tried both her ankles.

"No, no, it is nothing, do not be concerned, I am well, it was only… I slipped. I am sure all is well," Georgiana stammered, but as Mrs Annesley tried to help her to stand, she staggered, and would have fallen, but for her companion's arm.

Together, Colonel Fitzwilliam and Mrs Annesley got her seated on the grassy bank, while the others stood about, giving all sorts of suggestions, as people always do, and trying to think of anything useful they could do, when there was nothing. "I think she may have sprained her ankle slightly," Mrs Annesley said. "I am sure that nothing is broken."

"It seems unlikely," said Colonel Fitzwilliam. "It was not a great fall, and she landed on the grass. I would be very surprised if any bones were broken. But what is best to be done now?" However, at that moment, Georgiana again tried to stand up, and this time she succeeded. She was a pitiful sight, with her face scarlet, and tears streaming down her cheeks; it was clear that the accident had distressed her very severely.

"We must take her home," said Mrs Annesley.

"Yes, indeed," said the Colonel. "Can she walk as far as the carriage, do you think? Or should we try to carry her?" Georgiana, hearing this, immediately—though not very clearly—intimated that she could walk. Holding tightly to Anne's arm, she proceeded to do so, and they arrived with little difficulty, though slowly, at the place where the pony carriage had been left.

Once she was safely placed in the carriage, Mrs Annesley turned to Anne. "I am afraid, my dear Miss de Bourgh, that we must abandon you," she said. "If you would like, when we arrive I will send one of the grooms to drive you back to Pemberley. But for now, there is not room for a third person, and I must accompany Miss Darcy." Anne, who had already come to this conclusion, lost no time in assuring Mrs Annesley that she would be quite comfortable walking back with the others, and the carriage drove off, amid the usual volley of good wishes and recommendations.

After this, nobody seemed to wish to spend more time at the face. Mrs Annesley, as a parting gesture, had handed out the basket with the food and drink, and having sat down in the shade of some rowan trees and refreshed themselves, it was generally agreed that they should start the walk back. The Colonel went ahead with Mr Caldwell, and Mrs Caldwell and her son accompanied Anne. After half a mile, Anne began to stumble.

"Do you find it very difficult to walk, Miss de Bourgh?" Mrs Caldwell asked.

"No… yes… a little," Anne replied. "I am getting a good deal stronger, though I prefer to ride. The difficulty is that I have not been in the habit of walking very much, and have not the shoes for it. These shoes are not stout enough, and the soles do not keep the pebbles from my feet. "

"We can go as slowly as you wish," Mrs Caldwell replied.

"Come, Miss de Bourgh," said her son. "Do you take my arm. Is that better?" It was indeed: with the support of his arm, Anne could take some of the weight off her abused feet, and at once felt more comfortable.

"It is all downhill," Mrs Caldwell said. "That makes it a good deal easier. See, we are almost at the park entrance already."

"But there is another mile and a half to go," Edmund Caldwell objected.

"Do not be concerned, I shall do very well," Anne replied.

"It is a pity that you do not walk more," he said. "It is always so: the more people walk, the more strength they have."

"It is true, but at home, I was considered to be unwell. I only walked in the gardens, or went out in a carriage with my companion—the lady who looked after me. The walk to church, in good weather, was the farthest I ever got."

"The way gets easier after the next turning," Mrs Caldwell said. "Do you see that track to the right? The one that turns away just before the park gate, and winds up by the stream, among those rocks? That goes to Edmund's house. He does not live with us, you know; he has his own home."

"It is three and a half miles from here," he said, "up a very steep track, unsuited for carriages, and fit only for riding. I would not recommend you to walk up there, Miss de Bourgh. It is very hard. There is a carriage way up the other side, from Burley."

"But perhaps we might make an expedition sometime; the house is worth seeing," Mrs Caldwell said. "It is quite an historic place, though it is old and shabby, and he has never fitted it up properly, because he lives there as a bachelor."

"It is true," her son said. "I rough it in two rooms, and the rest of the house is pretty well empty."

"And I think," said his mother, "that he lives on bread and ham."

"Oh, come, Mother, it is not so bad as that. Old Murray's wife is quite a good cook; they look after me very well."

"It will be very pleasant when it is done up—and you will, sometime," his mother said. "The rooms are all done up in the old paneled style, Miss de Bourgh, which they call linenfold, and it is rather dark."

"But I think you might like to see it, Miss de Bourgh," her son said. "It was built by recusants—people who wanted to go on practising the old Catholic religion, in Queen Elizabeth's time. They wanted to live in a retired place, for their religion was forbidden. But they needed to see who was coming, and there is one room upstairs that has three windows, with views down several valleys. I have always thought it would be a wonderful room for a painter, or for an author to write in."

"What happened to them?" Anne asked.

"Oh, they were ruined by the fines, for if people did not go to church, they were made to pay, so the queen got rich and they got poor. In the end, the house was sold and they went to live overseas, in France, and never came back."

"That is a sad story."

"Yes, it is," said Edmund. "I often feel sad for those people, ruined for practising what they believed in."

"But... is it not very wrong, to be a Roman Catholic? I was always taught so."

"But then, is it not wrong to punish people for their beliefs? And what about those people, who truly believed that they must teach this belief to their children, and no other?"

"Now," said Mrs Caldwell, laughing, "you have done something, Miss de Bourgh, that no Caldwell can resist. You have started an argument."

"Say rather, a discussion," said her son. "Do not be afraid, Miss de Bourgh, we will not get angry." And, discoursing of religious beliefs, and houses, and history, they reached Pemberley in very good time, and Anne found that she was not tired at all! Walking, she thought, did agree with her, especially when it was done in the company of Mr Edmund Caldwell.

Georgiana, they learned, had scraped her hands, and bruised her knee, but there was no sign of a sprain, and it seemed that the pain she had experienced must have been due to the shock of the fall. Most importantly, she would not be prevented from going to the Lambton assembly, which was shortly to take place.

Chapter 11

E ACH MORNING, ANNE WOULD RIDE. COLONEL FITZWILLIAM WAS very pleased with her, and she found riding far less tiring than walking, allowing her to see more of the park.

One morning, a few days after the walk to the rock face, when the two of them got back, they learned that Mrs Caldwell had gone out driving with Mrs Darcy, but since the pony carriage would only hold two, the others had decided on a walk. Darcy, it seemed, had business letters that would not wait. Colonel Fitzwilliam said he would follow the walking party and catch them up. Anne was disinclined to walk, and went to Georgiana's room to practise at the piano. She had but just begun, when the butler approached her and murmured, "A person to see you, miss."

"Who is it, Forrest?"

"I understand he is your respected mother's agent, miss."

"Oh! very well, I will see him."

The agent was in the library. "Good day, Mr Colby."

"Good day, miss. I was expecting…"

"Yes, of course; you were expecting to see Lady Catherine. Well, she is at Burley; she was taken ill, you see, on the way here."

"Yes, miss, so I understand from Mr Forrest. I shall go there, of course. I will be on my way—but there is just one thing, since you are here, miss. It is regarding the usual business at this time of year," and, smiling kindly, he withdrew from his case a pile of papers. "If you would just sign over the income, as per usual, your signature is wanted here, and here…"

Anne looked at the papers. "What is this, Colby?"

"Why, miss, you sign it every year, it is just as usual."

"Yes, but what do I sign? I think I should read it, first."

Mr Colby looked a little agitated. "Lady Catherine wishes it signed, ma'am."

"But I am not sure that I should sign it, without understanding what is in it."

"There is nothing different, miss, you sign it every year."

"Well, that may be so, but I think I should not have signed it, without understanding it."

"It is just your name, miss, and it makes over the income."

Anne began to feel confused, and frightened. Mr Colby seemed so sure; why was she being so stupid? It must be right, to sign; but why could she not know what she was doing?

Just at that moment, Mr Edmund Caldwell came in. "Oh! Excuse me, Miss de Bourgh. I was looking for Darcy."

"I believe he is in his study," said Anne; and he made to leave. Suddenly she called out "Oh! pray, Mr Caldwell, do not leave, pray help me."

He came back into the room. "What is the matter, Miss de Bourgh?"

"It is only… Mr Colby has brought this document for me to sign, and I do not know… I do not understand… I am sure it is right, but should I sign something I do not understand?"

"Certainly not," he replied, calmly. "Mr… Colby, is it?… that seems to be a legal document that you have there; can you not explain its nature to Miss de Bourgh?"

"Oh, sir," the agent replied, smiling patronizingly, "young ladies do not want to understand the intricacies of such things, young ladies and legal language do not mix."

"Then young ladies will be swindled, as older people have been before them," Mr Caldwell replied, holding out his hand for the papers. He perused the top ones swiftly.

"This seems to be a document handing something over three hundred pounds into Lady Catherine's keeping," he said. "How comes this about, that Miss de Bourgh should be in possession of such a sum? And this being the case, why should she be expected to surrender it? Do you know anything about this, Miss de Bourgh?"

"No, sir."

"Excuse me, sir," the agent said, "but this is a private family matter, and…"

"You are right," said Mr Caldwell. "It is a family matter, and Miss de Bourgh needs the advice of a member of her family," and ringing the bell, he ordered the butler. "Request Mr Darcy to come here immediately. Miss de Bourgh is in distress, and needs him." The butler disappeared. "Oh, do not leave me," Anne whispered, almost ready to sink. "Do not be afraid, Miss de Bourgh," he said. "I will not leave until Mr Darcy arrives," and, taking her to an armchair, he compelled her to be seated, and sat down opposite her in silence, smiling reassuringly at her, until her cousin appeared, whereupon he quietly left the room.

Mr Darcy quickly ascertained the situation, as far as Mr Colby understood it. Sir Lewis de Bourgh had, it appeared, in a codicil to his will, left money in trust to provide a personal income for his beloved daughter, for her use until such time as she should marry, when a proper provision was to be made. The income, it seemed, was to have been handed over to Anne at each anniversary. Instead, Lady Catherine had always insisted—from no better motive, it seemed, than that love of controlling and dictating that ruled her life—on its being paid over to her, to be used on Anne's behalf. Anne, understanding little of what was happening, since nobody explained it to her, had always signed it away. There was nothing improper about this arrangement, since Anne had always agreed to it; but if she did not like it, she was at liberty, said Mr Darcy, to change it, and have the use of her own money: "For it is her money, is it not, Mr Colby?"

"Yes indeed, sir," said the agent, "But Lady Catherine wanted…"

"It is a case," said Mr Darcy, "of what my cousin wants. What do you want, Anne?"

Anne took a deep breath. "I want to have the money, sir."

Mr Colby said, "But where do you want it assigned, miss? Are you asking to have the capital, which is in trust, or the interest? Do you have a banking account?"

"No, but…"

"Do not be afraid, cousin," said Mr Darcy. "Mr Colby, my cousin is five-and-twenty years old, she is not a child. Why do we not take this matter elsewhere, and see to it together that the money is put into an account at a bank, in her name, and I will myself instruct her in the use of it. Cousin Anne, will you allow me to act for you in this matter?"

"Oh, yes, cousin, if you please."

"Very good, it shall be done. Come, Mr Colby." And he led the agent from the room.

Chapter 12

A S SOON AS SHE WAS ALONE, ANNE WENT TO A SECLUDED CORNER, where there stood a writing table, with a comfortable chair placed beside it. Set beside a window, it commanded a fine view over the park and stream, and in the past couple of weeks she had taken to using it every day. Whatever books she was reading, the writing upon which she was engaged, always lay there undisturbed, and she had come almost to regard it as her own. Here she sat, waiting for her cousin to return, and trying to understand what had happened. Her mind was in turmoil.

She had defied her mother; she had disregarded her expressed wishes!

She hoped her cousin would return soon; she needed to talk to him—or, rather, she needed him to talk to *her*, to explain, to tell her that she had not done something wicked. How strange that she, who had feared and disliked her cousin, should now be regarding him as a protector! He had changed so much, since his marriage; a happy husband, and soon to be a father. But he could not protect her from her mother's anger. She had accepted her cousin as her authority, rather than her mother—and Lady Catherine was already angry with Darcy, so angry that, as Anne knew, she had not wanted to come to Pemberley at all, and only desperation had driven her to it. Yes, thought Anne, desperation to get me married—not to someone who would love me and cherish me, but to someone who would be useful to her! But one could not hate a parent—one could not disobey. Affection, obedience were owed to a parent. Even, wondered Anne, if that parent had no knowledge, no understanding of one's needs?

But before Darcy came, Edmund Caldwell had helped her. She could not have stood up to Mr Colby, she would simply have done as she was bid, if he had not been there. How kind he had been, how steady! Edmund was no hero: stocky, by no means handsome, never well dressed, he cut no figure beside the elegant Darcy, or the soldierly Colonel Fitzwilliam. Yet when he had entered the room, she had immediately had the sense, in the middle of her confusion, that here was someone with whom she was safe. And she had been; she must thank him. But he could not keep her mother away from her. She remembered with a shudder her mother's rage when she had discovered that Cousin Darcy was indeed going to marry Elizabeth; her furious ill-temper with her household; how she had railed at Mr and Mrs Collins; and then had learned, to her fury, that Mr Collins could not be put out of his living.

Then she thought, *But then I was ill. Then I had no money. And Mr Collins could not be put out.* It had all died down, and between the lady of the manor and the parish priest an uneasy peace had descended. Civility, if not friendship, had been restored. When people must live together, Anne thought, they do.

Now she was well. Now, suddenly, she had money. How miserable could her mother make her, when she could still learn to play the piano, for now she could pay for a master? When she could hire a maid for herself? *I will buy myself some new dresses, of my own choosing,* she thought. *I will buy myself a horse, and ride it!*

But I do not want to go back to Rosings. Oh, why does my cousin not come?

In the end, it was Georgiana who came to find her. The walking party had returned, she said, "And there is a cold collation in the dining room, and there is a visitor as well, whom I think you will like."

"Is it Lady Louisa Benton?" Anne asked, for she knew her mother's friend was expected that day.

"No, she is not here yet, but it is Elizabeth's papa, Mr Bennet. I do not like her mama so very much, but he is the greatest dear, so droll. He always turns up when we do not expect him. And Anne, he has come from Longbourn, to give us the news that Elizabeth's sister, Mrs Bingley, has been brought to bed, and she has a little girl. Come, you must come!"

They found the party in the dining room gathered round the table, and with them a small, elderly, bright-eyed gentleman in a long, grey travelling coat. Elizabeth was happily perusing a letter, apparently from her mother: "Jane is well, very well, and the baby is to be called Elizabeth Caroline. Caroline Bingley and I are asked to stand godmothers, and the godfather will be a Mr Robinson, a school friend of dear Bingley."

"Oh, why not my brother?" cried Georgiana.

"They are saving him for a boy," said Mr Bennet.

"But tell us more, papa! What does it look like? Whom does it resemble? Mama says it looks like dear Bingley, but do you think so?"

"Oh, I do not know. It is either a boy, or a girl, and it looks like a baby; that is, there are a great many long clothes, and nothing much else. Bingley allowed the lease to expire, you know, on Netherfield, for he thought they would be in this part of the world, in their new home, long before the child was born. He would—he always expects that things will be for the best. But it was not so, and the new people wanted to get in, so he and Jane came to stay with us. I do not know when we will get them out. I came away because the women were making such a cackle, you could get no sense from any of them."

"You mean, you could get no attention, sir," said his son-in-law, laughing. "But things will be no better here, you know, within a few weeks."

"Well, well, I think, my dear sir, that you will retain a few shreds of good sense; and my daughter Elizabeth has more of quickness about her than my other girls. Whatever happens, your library is bigger than mine; I shall be able to retire into my own small corner, and get away from the noise."

"Come to us, sir," said Mr Caldwell. "We will take you walking in the hills, and tell you all about our fossils, and our remarkable curiosities."

"But it will be such a happy event!" said Mrs Caldwell, not quite understanding.

They were all talking; they were all laughing. She could not get to her cousin; she could not get to Edmund. Anne's head ached, she could eat nothing; she could feel sickness coming on. Suddenly she heard kind Mrs Annesley's quiet voice: "Miss de Bourgh, I think you are not quite well. Come, let me take you upstairs, you should lie down on your bed." Georgiana jumped up immediately, and insisted on taking her to her room, and got her maid. The housekeeper herself brought her up some lime leaf tea. She lay down; she slept.

Later that afternoon, she woke. She felt quite well, and when she came downstairs, Mr Darcy took her on one side. "As far as Mr Colby and I can ascertain," he said, "the original sum provided by your father must have been five thousand pounds. In the usual way, that would have given you an income of two hundred and fifty pounds—a very proper provision for a young woman of your rank, coming out into the world, to buy her clothes, etc, and get used to the handling of money."

"Two hundred and fifty pounds!"

"Wait, there is more. In the normal way, that would have been the case; as it was, your mother decided to continue living at Rosings, you were never presented at Court, or brought out into society, and you never had the use of the money. With the interest never being spent, but always added back into the capital, the original amount—how long ago was it, when your father died?"

"Ten years ago. I was fifteen years old, and am now five-and-twenty."

"Yes, we thought so. In that time, you see, the capital has increased to well over seven thousand pounds, and the income to almost four hundred: three hundred and eighty-seven, to be exact. Of course, you understand that, once you begin spending the interest, the capital will not increase."

Anne was not sure that she understood anything! The situation, her cousin reflected, was an excellent lesson in the power of compound interest, but was completely outside the range of Anne's knowledge and experience. The cottager's child who takes a shilling to the baker's, and brings home the change in pennies, he thought, probably knows more about money than she does.

However, Anne surprised him.

"Cousin, I must learn to keep track of my money. How can I do so? I might write a sort of list of the things I would like to buy, and how much they might cost. Do you think that would help me? If I do that, will you look it over for me?"

"Certainly. In fact, I have a better idea, which is that you should consult with Elizabeth. From being brought up in a family that is not rich, she has a far better idea of the planning and spending of income than either Georgiana or I—she knows, for example, how much clothes ought to cost—and I know she will be happy to assist you. And if you wish, I will be your banker until an account is arranged for you. Would you like to have something now, to be going on with?" he asked. "Would twenty pounds suffice?"

Twenty pounds! It was more money than she had ever seen!

"And when you have your bank account, you can write me your first draft, to repay me. One other matter: Edmund Caldwell must go home tomorrow, his business does not allow him to be longer away. I have arranged for Fitzwilliam to ride with him, and go into Burley to visit your mother. It is time one of us went and enquired after her health. While he is there, he will talk to her about this business. Trust me, he will get her approval. She likes Fitzwilliam, and he can usually get her to see things from his point of view. But for now, this must wait. I see a carriage coming up the drive."

Chapter 13

L ADY LOUISA WAS A KIND AND SENSIBLE WOMAN. SHE HAD BEEN a close friend of Lady Anne Darcy, and for her sake, held her son and daughter in affection. She had never been as fond of Lady Catherine, though she corresponded with her regularly, and Anne she hardly remembered. She had come to Pemberley out of concern for Georgiana. Mr Darcy, in his letter of invitation, had hinted that it was time Georgiana was thinking of a husband, and that there seemed to be few suitable young men available. Lady Louisa, from a wealth of experience, wondered if an unsuitable one were in the picture.

Now, she realized, the picture was complex. It did not take her five minutes to recognize Georgiana's admiration for Colonel Fitzwilliam, and to discount it; the colonel, at his age, was not likely to fall in love with a young girl. Nor, if he did so, would he think it right to persuade his wealthy cousin to marry him. Georgiana was young enough, she would get over it; but another admirer or two would certainly help. And, if she were in the habit of falling in love (there had been rumours), it would be as well to get her suitably married as soon as might be.

Anne was another matter; her mother had described her as sickly and frail, but she was nothing of the kind. However, she was five-and-twenty if she was a day. Catherine was a great fool, Lady Louisa thought, to let her hang around all those years after Darcy, who anybody could see would only marry a woman of the greatest charm and beauty, a woman to sweep him off his feet. This was not such a girl, though she would not make a bad wife, either. Edmund Caldwell obviously thought so, but that was no use—he could not aspire to the heiress of Rosings and thirty thousand pounds. Lady Louisa began making a list of the men she knew—not too young— deserving of Anne and thirty thousand pounds. It was a quite encouraging list, and she decided to give a ball within the next few weeks.

The evening was warm and sultry. Dinner was late, and afterwards, everyone was too hot for dancing. The doors of the drawing-room opened on the terrace, and at first everybody strolled about, feeling listless; presently they were all assembled inside. "Would Miss Georgiana play for them?"

Georgiana played two or three pieces, but seemed disinclined for more. Then Mr Bennet quietly said, "If the company would like it, I will read to you." Everyone expressed an inclination—to be read to was the very thing, for all they need do was sit, and listen.

Mr Bennet began, reading from some papers in his lap. It was an historic tale—a prose story, written in such a vein as to be almost poetry; a tale of a castle by moonlight, and a young girl waiting, sadly, for someone who did not return. The water fell plashing into the fountain, the white roses bloomed, the young girl wept. When Mr Bennet stopped, Georgiana drew a deep breath, and Mrs Caldwell wiped away a tear.

"Who wrote it?" was the question on everybody's lips, and "Was there more?"

"Papa," said Elizabeth, "you do not usually read romantic tales— where had you such a story?"

"Why, my dear," said Mr Bennet, "did you not write it? I found it on my table in the library, and thought that you had put it there for me to see."

"No indeed," said Elizabeth, "I never wrote anything in my life, longer than a letter; and surely the handwriting is not mine."

"All women," said her father, "write the same vile hand."

"The story is mine," Anne said shyly. "I left the sheets on a table in the library; I did not know, sir, that the table was yours."

There was immediate clamour. They had an authoress in their midst—how long had she been writing? Why had she said nothing? How did the story continue? And how did it end?

"I have written for years," said Anne. "I had a governess who recommended to me the copying of extracts, to improve my handwriting. I found it very dull copying other people's writings, and began to invent my own: little stories, poems, essays. Then I read a couple of novels and thought them rather silly. I thought I could do as well, and just to amuse myself, I began that story."

"And how does it go on?"

"Oh, she runs away to the Crusades, and has all kind of adventures. It is all nonsense."

"But, we must hear it!"

"One moment," said Mr Bennet. "Miss de Bourgh has been imposed on; I would not have read these pages, if I had known whose work they were. Only she can decide whether to allow us to hear more."

What authoress is really reluctant to have her story read to an admiring, encouraging crowd? Anne took the manuscript, and began to read. It was a strange feeling to be reading what she had written. All eyes were upon her; but her confidence increased as she read. After three or four chapters, her voice grew thick. "Come," said Mrs Darcy, "the rest must be for other evenings, it is too late now. The Lambton assembly is tomorrow," and the party broke up. Anne was thanked and praised; everyone wanted to hear more. Only Edmund Caldwell was silent.

But it was hard for Anne to sleep. Mr Caldwell and the Colonel were to leave the house as soon as they had breakfasted the next morning. She felt an urgent need to thank Mr Caldwell for his kindness to her the previous day; she could not let him go without thanking him. And yet she dared not ask him for an interview—it would look so particular! As far as she knew, her cousin had told nobody the story—except the Colonel, who, after all, was also a cousin—and somehow she knew that Edmund had not mentioned it to anybody. Suppose she were to sleep late, and he were to leave before she could speak to him? The maid who waited on her had been told to call her, but maids were often unreliable... Anne tossed and turned until it seemed to her that dawn was breaking, and then suddenly there was a voice calling her, and the maid had remembered after all.

There was, in fact, no difficulty; he was standing on the terrace, looking at the view. She tried to put her thanks into words; he cut her short.

"What I did was nothing, and I have no right to assist you; I wish I had. But there is something I wish to say to you," he said. "Your cousin will have told you this already, but I will repeat it. I read that document; you have every right to your own money, and your mother, however good her intentions, was wrong to withhold it. The matter would be different, of course, if your mother were in any danger of financial hardship; but that is certainly not the case. And even then, she should not have withheld, without asking, money which belongs to you. We all have obligations to a parent, but as we grow into adulthood, our responsibilities change; we owe respect, affection, but not blind, unthinking obedience. We have duties, which a parent cannot forbid us to perform. You are responsible for your money, and it is your task to decide how it should be used. Do not ever allow anyone to tell you, as that man did, that 'young ladies' have no need to think, or no right to learn. Never allow anyone to do your thinking for you."

"No... no... I will remember. But..."

"But?"

"I do not know... Will you be at the assembly tonight?"

"No. I cannot."

"And you do not much care to dance, do you?"

"Not much. I can understand why people like to dance, but I am clumsy; the music does not speak to me as it does to some. I am not made for mirth. But you love to dance, do you not?"

"Not as much as Georgiana; I like it, but I am soon tired."

"You must exercise more, then you will not get tired."

"But I am learning to ride."

"That is very good," said he, smiling, "but you must walk a little, too, every day."

"Very well, I will try."

"Now I must be on my way. I must be about my business. I know, why cannot I stay—you must think me a money-grubbing fellow, and that is what I am.

"You see, Miss de Bourgh, there is something I must tell you. My parents had a good fortune, but some years ago, I persuaded them to enter into a doubtful speculation. I was young, I was foolish, I was misled by dishonest people, and they lost a great deal of money. It was my fault, and I must ensure that their fortune is restored. They are all goodness, they have never asked for anything or spoken a word of blame, but that is my responsibility. Our land is not profitable for farming, but the quarry has opened up a very good way of making money, and it gives employment to people, who would not otherwise have work. I chose to employ local men, rather than bring in outsiders, but they are not used to the work, and they require constant attention and supervision. This is why I must go, when I would much rather stay. It may be many years before I have the money to be leisured."

"I see."

"Goodbye."

"Goodbye, sir... Mr Caldwell!"

"Yes, ma'am?"

"Thank you for telling me about... about... I understand your situation, and I honour you for it."

He turned to go; turning back, he raised her hand to his lips, and kissed it. Then he was gone.

Chapter 14

M RS DARCY, USED TO LIVING AMONG A LARGE NUMBER OF
sisters, was really rejoiced to have Anne staying with her, and
equally glad to have Lady Louisa and the Caldwells in her home for
the night of the Lambton assembly. She enjoyed the happy bustle
of the day before a ball.

"The Assembly Rooms are almost outside our gates," she told
her husband. "You can have no fears for me. I shall not dance, but
I do wish to go."

"I only wondered," he said, "if you and Mrs Annesley would like
to stay behind. I will tell you what I do fear, and that is, bringing
six women to an assembly, and only one man. I have only Caldwell.
Fitzwilliam and Edmund Caldwell have left us, and your father
refuses to go."

"I know; he never would go to the dances at Meryton. But my
mother brought all five of us, and there was always a shortage of
gentlemen as a result. Do you remember the evening that we met?
I could not get a partner, and was sitting down. That is why I overheard you, when you were so ungallant as to refuse to dance with
me. I know now, of course, the reason for your bad temper: you were
just come from dealing with the abominable Wickham," she said.

"If you remind me of *that,* I can refuse you nothing. In any case, poor Mrs Annesley should not be required to forgo an evening's enjoyment, merely to suit my requirements."

"She is an excellent person, is she not? I thought that we would not need her, but she is so good-tempered, so useful. Georgiana still needs a music instructress, and Anne is enjoying her lessons, too."

"Yes, indeed. In any case, I do not like to dismiss a person who has given us such good service, for who knows whether she would get another post? And besides, my love, in a very few years' time, we will need a governess, will we not?"

In view of her husband's anxiety, however, Mrs Darcy agreed to stay quietly at home for the morning, and allow Mrs Annesley and Georgiana to take Anne into Lambton, to buy a new pair of dancing sandals, and a few other necessities for the evening.

This was enough to spread the news around the town that a large party from Pemberley would be at the assembly. Some said Mr and Mrs Darcy would bring ten women, and eight men, others said there would be six women and five men, but it was generally known that an heiress would be among the party, and someone pointed out that it was twice as good as the first report, for, if one counted Miss Georgiana Darcy, that made two.

Lambton had some excellent shops, and what with the buying of new gloves, and inspecting Georgiana's purchases, and approving of them, the morning flew away. It was just as well, thought Anne, for she had not time to think, and she was not sure that she wanted it.

But a mind like hers, used to solitude, must and will find it. In the course of the afternoon, she found herself at the table in the corner of the library that she had come to regard as hers. Mr Bennet had categorically refused to take it, saying that authors were privileged people, and that all the reward he claimed was the pleasure of hearing more of her story: "The place is enormous, and there are at least half a dozen very comfortable armchairs, where I can sleep in peace," he told her; and he told his daughter, "I would even let Miss de Bourgh into my own library at home, for I will guarantee that she does not chatter, or disturb one by wanting a pen mended, or an argument settled. She is a very uncommon young woman."

"There is more to her than any of us thought," Elizabeth replied. "Who would have thought that she had such an imagination? Such a power of telling a story?"

But this afternoon, Anne's mind seemed empty. She could not write a line; she could not review what she had written previously; she could not even read. All she could think of were Edmund's words, Edmund's look, Edmund's gesture.

He had kissed her hand. Men did not commonly kiss a woman's hand; she had never known such a thing. Taken in conjunction with what he had told her, it was as if he were saying goodbye. A farewell. She knew it, and she knew why: *he loves me, and I love him.*

It would never do. She knew it; and she understood it was his way of telling her that he knew it, too. His lack of rank, his restricted means, his occupation, not to mention his egalitarian ideas, all would make him unacceptable to her mother. Lady Catherine would refuse even to be introduced to him. Darcy too, she thought: even though he had married a penniless woman, of lower rank than his own, and liked Edmund as a friend, he would not welcome him as a cousin. It was very well for a woman to marry above her station, but for a man to seek to wed a woman of higher rank, and great wealth, with nothing to offer in return, would be regarded as fortune-hunting of the meanest description. Edmund would never do it. Rosings was hung around her neck, a burden she could never escape. Her wealth, instead of giving her freedom, would forever imprison her.

Musings like this kept her miserably occupied until Mrs Annesley came to find her. "My dear Miss de Bourgh," she cried. "What is the matter? You are quite pale. And the assembly tonight! You have the head-ache; you have been reading, you have been writing too long!" Anne had no wish to explain the real reason for her wan looks, and allowed Mrs Annesley to persuade her to take a gentle turn around the grounds, and even to walk as far as the stream, which made her feel much better.

The evening was fine, and the drive pleasant. As they went down the hill through the little town, Mrs Darcy exclaimed, "Oh, my dear, we forgot to find a tenant for the White Cottage."

"I did not forget," Darcy said, "but I like to rent it to someone connected with the family, and there is no one, at the moment, answering that description. I want a good tenant, for it is a pretty place." The carriage was stopped so that they could see it. It was, indeed, pretty. It stood a little back from the street, separated from it by a small garden, with a good-looking orchard behind.

"Rent it to me," Anne suddenly said. "It is just the sort of little place I should like. I will live there, cousin, and write books." Everyone laughed.

By the time they got there, the rooms were beginning to fill. It was pleasant to see the kind of stir, the whispering, the smiles of gratification, as the word spread through the room that the party from Pemberley was come. Anne, who had been used to stiffness, embarrassment, and forced cordiality, suddenly realized that her dress was pretty, her jewels exquisite, and her hair very well dressed, and that these people were pleased to meet her. She was introduced here and there; she was asked to dance again and again; and greatest of wonders, she had no difficulty in dancing, for her partners were so kind and forbearing! She hardly had time to think, and her spirits lifted, in spite of her distress. A ball was indeed delightful!

She soon noticed that Georgiana was not enjoying herself. At first, Anne thought she was missing Colonel Fitzwilliam, but she quickly realized that Georgiana was simply shy in a large company. She did not know how to reply to well-meant commonplaces, and was uncomfortable with those of lower rank. Her manner was stiff; she looked haughty, even plain. Anne remembered what it was like to be young, and trying to make a good appearance to strangers. There was something to be said, she thought, for being five-and-twenty years old.

After several dances, Anne found herself without a partner, and felt tired. Mrs Darcy was sitting at the side, talking comfortably to her neighbours. Seeing an empty chair beside her, Anne went to sit down. Elizabeth said, "We miss Colonel Fitzwilliam, do we not?"

"Indeed, cousin," Anne said. She realized that she had not given him a thought; nor had she thought of his errand to her mother. The whole day, in every leisured moment, her thoughts had been with Edmund Caldwell: *He cannot marry—he meant to tell me that he cannot marry, not for many years; that he cannot marry me… I will live there, and write books…*

"Anne, I have made three unexceptionable remarks, and you have not answered," Mrs Darcy said. "I admit that they were all three very dull—but is something amiss?"

"Oh, no," Anne said. "No, not at all… Oh, Elizabeth, who is that girl that Georgiana is talking to? Do but look at her!"

Both looked. Miss Darcy was standing talking to a pretty girl, and the change in her manner was remarkable. They were too far away to hear anything, but Georgiana was smiling, she was laughing, she was clasping the other girl by the hand, and the flush on her cheeks spoke of happiness.

Elizabeth turned to her neighbour. "Who is that, Mrs Hatherley, the young lady in the blue muslin?"

"It is Miss Rackham, ma'am; that is her brother, dancing with Mrs Shipton. His mama is sitting down, over there; she is a widow."

"Of course, we were introduced just now," said Mrs Darcy. "So those are her children."

"They are but just come into the country. His uncle was old Sir William, a sad invalid, at Wharton Place, you know, ma'am. He died a few weeks ago, and this young man has inherited the title and the property, but they say it is in a terrible state, for the old gentleman did nothing to it. He is not at all handsome, but a very pleasant, well-spoken young man."

But she had not time to say more, for Georgiana came over to them, bringing the pretty girl, and introduced her.

"She was at school with me," she explained. "I was homesick, and Mary was so kind to me. It was the horridest place you can think of. I became sick, and then my dear brother came and took me away, but Mary was sick, too, at the same time, and I never got her direction—and here she is!"

Arrangements were rapidly made: they were to ride together, to draw together, and as soon as the weather should be wet, to play the pianoforte together. As they drove away, Georgiana seemed a different girl, and Lady Louisa made up her mind, when she gave her own ball, to include the young Rackhams in her invitations.

Chapter 15

THE NEXT DAY, COLONEL FITZWILLIAM RETURNED. LADY
Catherine, he said, was well and in good spirits, and sent
proper messages to everyone. Sitting beside Anne, at their midday
cold collation, he quietly told her, "I had no trouble in bringing
her round, cousin, over the matter of your inheritance."

"I thought she would be very angry. How did you do it?"

"I told her how wise she was, to do as she has done. I told her
that she had shown very good judgment in entrusting you now
with the bequest, for she obviously knew the difficulties that young
women, with no experience in handling money, often have when
they marry; and I reminded her that at that point there will be a large
fortune to be managed. I happened to mention this in the Pump
Room, in the company of her friends, who smiled, and agreed, and
mentioned several instances of young married women of very good
families who had run into debt. She could hardly admit, in front
of them, that she had been forced into doing what she did; and
she did not at all object to their being reminded that she is a very
wealthy woman. Now she regards it, first, as a settled thing, second,
as a thing admired by people she respects, and third, as something
she thought of herself. I am an army man, remember," he said,

smiling. "There are tricks that work very well when one is dealing with senior officers."

The conversation became general, and he explained that he had stayed overnight in order to dine, at his aunt's invitation, with the Duchess of Stilbury, and her brother, Lord Francis Meaburn. Lady Catherine, he said, was in very good spirits; and, he added, was dressed exactly like the Duchess, that is, in the very latest fashion. He thought her petticoats might be a little thicker than was generally worn, but she had a huge poke bonnet, and a pair of black and yellow boots. She and the Duchess were the best of friends, and the rest of the town, both visitors and residents, looked up to them with awe. "I should like to know what Meaburn thinks of it all, though," he said. "He is not the kind of man to sit down in a small spa town, drinking the waters and going to bed at eleven, because he loves his sister; he is more of a Brighton man."

"I fancy," Darcy said, "that money might have something to do with it."

"I think it has everything to do with it," agreed Fitzwilliam. "He was a Colonel in the—th, you know. I know some of the officers in that regiment, and I remember they told me that his extravagance was unbelievable. Eventually he was forced to sell out, because his gaming debts were so huge."

"Did he not marry Lord W——'s daughter?"

"He did. They say he had run through all her money by the time she died. But tell me, cousin, what has become of Dawson? There was a sour-faced woman in her place. Did she leave your mother's employment?"

"Yes, indeed," said Anne. "If you remember, whenever we went anywhere my mother would have her sit on the box, and she was always quite willing. As it turned out, she was in love with the coachman; we could hear the two of them, laughing. Then he left, and she eloped with him. My mother does not like to have new people around her, so she promoted Mullins, who was the sewing maid before. I was sorry, for Dawson was very good-natured, and Mullins is not."

The languor of the day after a ball was being felt; Lady Louisa had left, and no one wanted to walk. They were sitting on the terrace, when a servant came and said that Mrs Caldwell was wanted. She returned looking rather flustered.

"My dear," she said to Anne, "there is something—I do not know what you will think, but my son has sent a gift for you. But he says that if you do not like it, it is to be sent back."

"A gift for Anne?" said Georgiana. "But what is it? And where is it?" and they looked round, expecting to see a parcel.

"It must be a book," said Anne, trying to speak calmly. "We were speaking of several titles that—but he offered to lend them—there is no need, Mrs Caldwell, I will return it."

"No," said Mrs Caldwell, "it is not a book. It is—it is in the stable yard. And if—if Mr and Mrs Darcy do not quite like it, it is to be sent back."

By this time, the curiosity of the rest of the party had been thoroughly aroused, and everyone wanted to see the mysterious object. They all accompanied Anne to the stable yard, Mr Darcy enquiring rather anxiously if his friend had given his cousin a horse? A groom was standing there, holding a swathed bundle.

"Are you not Mr Caldwell's servant?" Mr Darcy asked. "Hinkins, is it not?"

"Yes, sir."

"Well, Hinkins, what have you got for us?"

The groom knelt down, opened the bundle, and put a small, white and brown puppy on the ground.

"Oh!" screamed Georgiana. "Oh! Anne!"

Anne fell on her knees. The little creature wagged its tail, and licked her hand. All the women made the kind of noises that ladies make, confronted with anything small and endearing. She patted it, and bent over it, trying to hide her face, for tears had sprung to her eyes.

"It be what they call a King Charles, sir," the groom said.

"It will not grow very large, will it?" Darcy asked.

"No, sir. Quite small, they are. Not near so big as a regular spaniel."

"And quite useless, I suspect."

"No good for hunting, sir, they be a lady's dog, like—a pet."

"A letter came, too," Mrs Caldwell said. "My son says, 'Tell Miss de Bourgh that she does not walk enough, and Minette will see to it that she takes a walk every day.'"

"But..." said Mrs Darcy, glancing doubtfully at her husband, "I do not know whether..."

Anne, still kneeling, looked up at her over the little creature's head. Elizabeth saw her face, saw her tears, and read the whole story in her eyes.

"I know about it," her husband said to her privately, later. "Caldwell came to me the morning he left. He has behaved very well. But I did not know, and neither, I think, did he, that it had gone so far with her."

"We cannot do other," Elizabeth said, "than let her keep the dog. It is the saddest thing!"

"I hate small dogs," Darcy said. "How could this happen? They have only known each other a week or so."

"I saw his face last night, while she was reading. And how long did it take you, to make up your mind about me?"

"I do not know. But I am sure that, after the ball at Netherfield, if I had not seen you again, it would all have been over. If you had not come to Hunsford while I was staying with my aunt…"

"So do you think," said Elizabeth, "that if they do not meet again, it will be forgotten?"

"Caldwell knows that it would be a most unsuitable match. If he has made up his mind, he will make no attempt to see her. As for her, I do not know."

"Nor I," said Elizabeth. "I think she is a girl who feels things very deeply; I think none of us knows her. But I know that this business has hurt her."

"I am sorry for it. But who could have known? I know one thing: I do not like the idea of sending her back to Rosings to pine. Perhaps her mother, even after she goes home, would allow Anne to make her home with us for a while. Meanwhile, this makes it all the more necessary to find someone suitable to marry her. A man of character would certainly not agree to go and live at Rosings, and Anne would have her own home, which is what she needs. Let me see, did not Sir Matthew Brocklebank dance with her the other night? He has no money, but there is the title, and he is a pleasant-looking fellow."

"But he can talk of nothing but horses," Elizabeth protested. "He never opens a book. If he knew that Anne is writing one, he would be too frightened to speak to her, let alone ask her to marry him."

"There was Mr Kirkman, he is bookish enough. A widower, but that might suit Anne very well; she is not so young, now. There are few men of five-and-twenty still unmarried."

"But she is becoming quite pretty, I think, with those large dark eyes and her chestnut hair. There is a bronze-green silk being made up for her, for Lady Louisa's ball; I think she will look quite lovely in it."

"How about that older brother who is staying at the Rectory with Mr Granby? He will inherit the baronetcy one day."

"Yes, and it would be pleasant to have her married to the Rector's brother," said Elizabeth. "But although Anne danced with all three of them, I do not believe she even noticed them. And meanwhile, I think we must let her keep the dog, for she needs something to love."

"I can see very well that Georgiana will want one, too. It is very unjust that a man should have his house filled with small animals, only because his cousin is crossed in love."

In view of the size of Pemberley, Elizabeth thought this something of an exaggeration, and said so.

"Oh, very well, very well; since she and Georgiana have been playing with the creature all evening, I suppose it must stay," Darcy said, resignedly. "It could be worse; at least Caldwell had the sense not to give her a pug."

Chapter 16

NOW THAT SHE HAD SOME MONEY, ANNE WAS ABLE TO BE generous with the servants, and it was not hard to find a footman who liked dogs, and was happy to care for Minette. Anne quickly learned the advantage of having a dog: she must walk now, whether she would or no; if the little creature did not have its exercise, it would not be healthy. Three days later, it was wet and showery; they did not ride, but Minette must have her walk. Anne came in, a little damp but smiling, to find that Miss Rackham had arrived to spend the day with Georgiana, and the Caldwells were making ready to depart.

"My dear," Mrs Caldwell said, "would you do us a very great favour? Would you lend us the sheets of your story, as far as has been read to this point? We will take very great care of them, and return them in a short while; but we would so much like to read them again."

Anne agreed readily, delighted to find that her story had such a power of commanding interest, and knowing that with such people as these, her precious manuscript would be safe. She would have liked to ask if Edmund might be interested to read it, but could not trust her voice in asking. She bade them farewell with real regret. *These people,* she thought, *would have been my family.*

Scarcely had the sound of their carriage ceased to be heard down the avenue, than the noise of another could be heard approaching. Anne, feeling that she wanted solitude, instantly resolved to take refuge in the library. Soon she was at her table, and Minette, dry and warm, was in the basket provided for her. Mr Bennet, with the same instinct, had made for his armchair; they never disturbed each other. But Minette would not stay in the basket, and whined to be picked up. Only to keep her quiet, Anne took the little dog onto her knee, and sat, stroking its warm, silky coat. She had seldom held a little creature like this before, and never for very long. The sensation was delightful. And Minette was her own, her very own! Only Edmund, she thought, could have made her such a perfect gift. Only Edmund... but her thoughts were interrupted. The butler approached: "If you please, miss, there are some visitors here, who are asking for you."

"Who is it, Forrest?"

"The Duchess of Stilbury, miss, and Lord Francis Meaburn. Mr and Mrs Darcy are with them, and Miss Georgiana, but they have asked for you especially."

"Of course, they are acquainted with my mother. I will come at once."

It was strange, but she felt perfectly capable, now, of meeting with complete strangers. Since she was the granddaughter of a nobleman, and the daughter of a Baronet, rank in itself did not particularly frighten her, and her improved health and looks had given her a confidence she had never previously known.

The Duchess, at least, was not the kind of person to inspire alarm, being merely a tall, large, silly-looking woman, dressed rather too fashionably for a visit to a country house in the daytime. But her brother was a different matter. Likewise tall, but much younger, fair-haired and handsome, he exuded an air of self-confidence that it might not be out of place to call arrogance, and also a slight, but detectable, air of dissipation and boredom. His sister obviously adored him.

Anne wondered if this was why Colonel Fitzwilliam, at least, looked uneasy; this was not the kind of man, she guessed, whom he liked to present to his female cousins. Colonel Fitzwilliam, she thought, having dined with them in Burley, has been forced into making the introduction. Georgiana and Miss Rackham looked frightened out of their wits. Elizabeth merely looked amused: Anne remembered that she had never, for a moment, shown awe, or even respect, for Lady Catherine; if the Duchess had tried to patronize Elizabeth, she had wasted her time. Cousin Darcy merely looked politely bored. After the introductions had been made in form, they all sat and looked at each other.

"You were in the library when we arrived, I believe, Miss de Bourgh," the Duchess said. "Are you a great reader? Are you a reader of novels, or do you despise them?"

"No indeed, I enjoy them very much," said Anne. She had a feeling that the Duchess would not like to hear that she was writing one. "But Mr Darcy has an excellent library on general topics as well, and I have been reading about the curious rocks and minerals of Derbyshire."

"Dear me! That sounds very serious. I never think that we poor women should tax our intellects too hard."

"It always seems very unfair to me," said Elizabeth, "that if a woman reads novels, she is called frivolous; and if she reads more serious works, she runs the risk of being called a blue-stocking."

"And if she reads nothing at all," said Darcy, "whatever she is called, she will be very stupid indeed." Anne had to bend her head to hide a smile.

After this, the conversation ranged, with amazing insipidity, from the weather, to the countryside, to the amenities of Burley, and Anne wondered why they had been so anxious to meet her. Perhaps they had brought a letter from her mother? But none was produced. Lord Francis, the introduction once made, barely spoke again. They moved into an adjoining saloon, where refreshments had been laid out; the refreshments were praised; the room was praised, the pictures on the wall were praised.

Eventually the visitors got up to leave, and the Duchess, smiling graciously, said, "You will see us again, you know, at Lady Louisa's ball; we shall be pleased to see you. She has not yet sent out her invitations, but do not be afraid, you are all asked, and we are very pleased. But your mother tells me you do not dance, Miss de Bourgh? Is that so?"

"No, madam," Anne replied. "It is not the case any more. There was a time, when I was in poor health, when dancing was too much for me, but I am recovered."

"I am afraid I may not be able to give you the meeting," Colonel Fitzwilliam said. "I am being recalled; I have had letters this morning."

"Well, we shall see the rest of you there. Goodbye," and she graciously held out her hand.

"Haw," said Lord Francis, speaking to her for the first time. "Haw. Dog. Little dog. You like dogs, Miss de Bourgh?"

Trying not to laugh, Anne said "I like this one, sir."

"Haw. So do I. Nice little creature."

"Thank you, sir."

"Glad you dance. Must dance with me, at the ball."

"Certainly, sir. Goodbye."

"Well," said Georgiana as soon as they had gone. "What was all that about? I was never so frightened in my life; and they did not seem to like us one bit. Why did they come? Cousin Fitzwilliam, are you really being recalled?"

"Certainly I am; did you think I would tell a lie? The Army has decided that it must take a look at me, and decide whether I am fit to go back and be shot at again, though they have not yet told me when they will send for me. I am quite ready, and I think I shall do very well. I need action; I miss my comrades. You have all been very good to me, but it is time to be gone. But tell me, Darcy: why do you think the Duchess and her precious brother came here? For they brought no message from Lady Catherine, not even a greeting. I have a very good idea that they came without Lady Catherine's knowledge."

"A thirty-mile drive, for the sake of an hour's visit," Darcy said. "Is our society really so desirable?"

"I am afraid that I may have done harm there," Fitzwilliam confessed. "I think my little stratagem for avoiding Lady Catherine's anger awakened these people to the fact that her daughter was staying in the neighbourhood. I think they knew before that Anne is a rich heiress, but did not know how rich; and in any case, assumed her to be sick, and at Rosings. I think they came here on what we would call in the Army a reconnaissance expedition; I think they came to take a look at you, Anne."

"Why Anne?" Mrs Darcy asked. "Why not Georgiana, too? She is just as much an heiress as Anne; they could see two of them, for the price of one."

"It could be a very good match," Darcy said. "Lord Francis has rank, good looks, and a splendid position in society, and he appeared good-natured. He would do for either of you."

"But he is old!" said Georgiana. "And he is so stupid!"

"I do not think him at all clever," said her brother, "but many clever, well-educated women marry stupid men, and are quite happy with them. His lack of money alone must make either of you acceptable to him; he could not do better. I shall not flatter your vanity by telling you that you are both pretty girls."

"And if he needs money as badly as they say," Elizabeth added, "he would probably be quite willing to marry both of you, if he were allowed."

"Well, that may be," said Georgiana. "He does seem very good-humoured. But I do not intend to marry an old, stupid man, however high his rank may be. I want to marry somebody young, who likes the things that I like. Do not you, Anne?"

"Yes, indeed," said Anne. "I think a similarity of ideas is the most important thing for happiness in a marriage, and surely a similarity of age must be part of that, for older men do not like the same things as young women."

"You are both of you far too nice," Darcy said. "If it were left up to you two, I do not know what would become of all the stupid men. Somebody must marry them, or what will become of us all?"

"I do not see that at all," said Elizabeth. "If nobody married any of them, the race of stupid men must die out."

"Well," said Georgiana, "however that may be, I am glad that I do not have to dance with Lord Francis. What shall you say to him, Anne? Haw? Haw?" and they all began to laugh.

Chapter 17

THIS ATTENTION FROM LADY CATHERINE'S ACQUAINTANCES brought something to Darcy's mind; he and Elizabeth both thought that it was time Anne paid a visit to her mother. Anne could not but agree with them; for a daughter to neglect her mother for any greater length of time would be unacceptable. The only wonder was that Lady Catherine had not written to request her presence.

"I think the reason is," said Colonel Fitzwilliam, "that she is really very happy in Burley. She is the most admired woman in the place."

"She used to be a handsome woman, I remember," Darcy said.

"Well, she looks splendid now that she is fashionably dressed; the Duchess and Lord Francis spend part of every day with her; the baths are doing wonders for her; and remember, she has not seen, as we have, the improvement in Anne's health—she thinks of her as a sickly, timid creature, who would find life at Burley too much, and be a disadvantage to her."

"Well, we must go; we cannot send Anne alone; some of us must go and see her," said Fitzwilliam, and the end of the week was quickly fixed upon for the expedition.

It only remained to decide who should go with Anne, to settle details of carriages, etc, and to write to the hotel to bespeak rooms for them all, for a fifteen-mile drive, each way, would consume far too much of the day. It must be an overnight stay at Burley; nay, two nights, for Saturday would be an assembly night, which would allow them the pleasure of attending the dance, and then they would stay over Sunday, and return on Monday.

Georgiana and Colonel Fitzwilliam said they would go, but Darcy felt he must stay at Pemberley with his wife. Mrs Annesley said she would stay, too, knowing that Lady Catherine would not have the slightest wish to meet her; but to everyone's surprise, Mr Bennet announced that he would accompany them. Of course, he said to his daughter, he was very much alarmed, but he could not resist the opportunity to write to Mr Collins and tell him that he had met Lady Catherine, and give him his impressions of her. Another consideration, he admitted to Anne, was that Darcy had told him that Burley possessed a bookstore, which was held to be remarkably well stocked.

They started early, and well before noon, were actually promenading round the Pump Room with Lady Catherine. She was, indeed, dressed in the height of the fashion, and in as good a mood as Anne had ever known, delighted with the attention, and strongly approving of Georgiana's looks, and quiet, ladylike demeanor. But her highest praise was reserved for her daughter. "I never saw you in better looks," she said, "and your health seems much improved, too."

"It is, indeed, madam."

"Well, now we must drink the water, for it does a great deal of good."

Anne had tasted the water already, and disliked it. She had hoped to do a little shopping, for, like Mr Bennet, she had her eyes on the famous bookstore. But Lady Catherine was already heading over to the pump. However, the plan of drinking the water was quickly overthrown, for at this moment the Duchess and her brother came into sight. If Lady Catherine had been genial before, she was effusive now, and so was the Duchess in her turn. "We seem to be witnessing a great meeting of minds," Mr Bennet observed quietly to Colonel Fitzwilliam.

"I think it is rather a great meeting of interests," the Colonel replied.

It had to be made clear, with a great deal of repetitious detail, that there was no need of introductions, for they had all met each other; and then the Duchess proposed a country walk. None of the other ladies had shoes for such an undertaking, but Her Grace's word was enough for Lady Catherine. She immediately agreed, and, no opportunity being given to anybody else to give an opinion, or ask to do anything different, they all presently found themselves walking up the main street, in the direction of the open country.

As they got into the older part of the town, the streets became narrow, and instead of stone pavements, they found themselves walking on old-fashioned cobblestones. The others were a little ahead, with Lady Catherine and the Duchess arm in arm. Turning around, the Duchess said, "Do take my brother's arm, Miss de Bourgh, the pavement is very uneven. Francis, give her your arm." Lord Francis seemed to have very little will-power of his own, but to leave every decision to his sister. He obediently extended an arm, and Anne took it, with Minette's leash on her left hand. *What on earth shall we talk about?* Anne wondered. But Lord Francis was equal to the challenge.

"Dog likes a walk," he said.

"Yes, she does."

"Nice little thing. Like bigger dogs, myself."

"Gentlemen mostly do, I believe, sir."

"Ha. Like a dog that can do something useful."

"I think you mean hunting, sir, do you not?"

"Ha. This little thing wouldn't be much use after a fox, heh?"

"I think the fox would chase her, sir."

"Haw, haw! Very good, Miss de Bourgh! The fox would chase her! Very good!" and Lord Francis threw back his head, and gave a loud, braying laugh. Anne, relieved at finding conversation so easy, looked up at him and laughed, too.

At that very moment, Edmund Caldwell came out of a side street, turned, and almost walked into them.

It was over in a flash. Anne had barely time for a startled glance, barely time to take her hand from Lord Francis' arm, and try to hold it out, but already he had sketched a bow, was past them, and gone down the street.

"Friend of yours?" Lord Francis said.

"A... an acquaintance sir."

"Seems to be in the devil of a hurry."

"Yes... yes... I think he did not see me."

"I tell you what, Miss de Bourgh, if I saw you in the street, I wouldn't run by you in such a hurry, by Jove, no, I would not."

Anne could have screamed with vexation!

That they should have met by such a chance, that they should have met at all—and then, not to be able to speak to him, to greet him, even! And that she should have been arm in arm with another gentleman—and this particular gentleman, as well—laughing with him, as though there were an understanding between them! Nothing could have been more unfortunate! Lord Francis went on talking—about what, she really had no idea, for she was saying "Yes," and "No, indeed," almost at random. They walked quite far into the countryside, far enough to return with weary ankles and spoiled shoes, but the magnificent scenery was wasted on Anne; she saw nothing, and it took her the rest of the day to recover her composure, and to reflect that, in the course of the next day, she might well meet Edmund, and would surely be able to rectify the misunderstanding.

If she had thought that Edmund might be there, the prospect of the assembly that evening would have held a good deal of suspense for her, but she knew that he would not be. Her best chance must be at church, on the following day—but then, what was she to say to him? "I do not really like Lord Francis, it was all a mistake"? Still, she would be at least able to greet him, to enquire after him, and of course his parents would probably be there, too; she could certainly talk to them… she must take care to come out of the church well behind her mother. She must dally a little, look at a tombstone or some such thing, so that with a little good luck, she might be able to greet him, to talk to him, to show him that she was still his friend!

This thought enabled Anne to enjoy the assembly. It was a far different affair from the Lambton assembly, where everybody knew everybody else, and many of those attending came from a quite modest sphere in life. Here, at a spa town, the company consisted, for the most part, of those wanting to make an impression on people they had, for the most part, never met before. Here, clothes were everything, for the eye is the easiest to impress, and many of those present had certainly spent more than they ought in the shops around the Promenade.

Happy was Lady Catherine, as she proceeded into the room, resplendent—nay, refulgent—in yellow satin, lace, and diamonds, and followed by two handsome young ladies, and two gentlemen. Mr Bennet had withstood, for twenty years, the arguments, the sighs, the pleadings of his wife, and never attended an assembly, but he was no match for Lady Catherine; she had forced him to attend. The Master of Ceremonies almost fell over himself in his deference, and his eagerness to greet them all. Even the Duchess and her brother did not command more attention. Lady Catherine did not dance, but she sat at the top of the room with the dancers circling below her, like the Presence itself. Anne danced a great deal, and Lord Francis danced with her twice, but she scarcely noticed her partners; she could only think of what the morrow might bring.

But all her conjecture was wasted: she did not see him at church. Arriving early, they were shown to a pew almost at the front. It was impossible to turn around, and look behind, and by the time they emerged, slowed up by the crush of people in front of them, most of the congregation had left. She tried to go to the evening service—Mrs Caldwell, she thought, might very probably be there—but she was prevented. "What are you thinking of, Anne?" her mother said. "You know that we are to drink tea with the Duchess," and she was obliged to sit there, for hours, and endure all the insipidity of the Duchess' conversation and Lord Francis' near-silence.

The next morning, no one seemed to be in a hurry to leave. At breakfast, Mr Bennet said, "If none of you object to waiting a little, I would be very glad to visit the famous bookstore." Anne, ready to leave, and wishing for some fresh air, said she would go with him: "They would only take a few minutes, they would be back almost at once," and on this understanding, the carriage was ordered, and Georgiana and the Colonel were happy to stroll around the Promenade with Lady Catherine. But who can take only a few minutes, in a bookstore? Anne was trying to decide which, of three beguiling new novels, she wished to buy, when she found herself addressed: "My dear Miss de Bourgh, how very pleasant to meet you here!" It was Mr Caldwell, Edmund's father.

She was delighted, and stammered a greeting and an enquiry after his family. Now she would hear, at least, how Edmund was. "We are all well, my dear, very well, and we have some news that I am sure will interest you," Mr Caldwell said. "We are losing Edmund; he is going away."

"Away? Why… how is this? Where? When?" Anne realized that she was stammering, and tried to bring her words into order. "You will certainly miss him… is it business that takes him? And when will he leave?"

"He is to set out for Barbados, in a month or so I am not precisely sure—he will go to Liverpool shortly, to enquire about a passage."

"Barbados? But that is…"

"It is in the West Indies. Yes, an island in the West Indies. Does that not sound interesting, Miss de Bourgh? He has been thinking about it for some time, and did not seem sure, but yesterday—no, yesterday was Sunday, it was Saturday, it was the day before yesterday, he came to us and said that he had made up his mind, he should go."

Mr Caldwell was delighted to tell her the particulars: the family had unexpectedly received word that they had inherited, from a distant kinsman, a property on the island, of which little was known except that it had been abandoned on the owner's death, and left unclaimed for some years. Edmund believed that something might be made of it; that he might live out there, and operate it; that at least it would pay him to go out there, see it, and if nothing could be done, make arrangements to sell it. His careful work on the quarry, he believed, had paid off; he could leave it under the control of a manager in whom he had confidence.

"His greatest concern," Mr Caldwell said, "is that, with his views, he could not contemplate the operation of the place by the use of slave labour, for it still goes on, you know, though it should not; the trade still continues, though there are laws against it. But Edmund wants to discover if he might not run the place using paid workers. It seems there are many white men there, who lost their employment years ago when the plantation owners went over to owning slaves, and have been living in poverty ever since. Is not that a dreadful thing, Miss de Bourgh?"

Alas! Anne could learn very little of all she wanted to know; Mr Caldwell was far more interested in the burning issue of slavery than in the material business of his son's journey. She was able to learn the approximate date of his departure, but then her companion called to her; even Mr Bennet was aware that they had spent too much time, and must leave. Taking a rapid farewell of Mr Caldwell, with only just enough time to send her warmest wishes to Mrs Caldwell, "…and my… my compliments to your son, if you please," she was forced to hurry away.

Chapter 18

THE FAREWELLS WERE CORDIAL, PROMISES WERE MADE TO COME back soon, it was a fine breezy day, and the journey back was a pleasant one. Anne heard nothing, saw nothing, and could not remember, later, in what terms she had taken leave of her mother. All the way back, she could think of nothing but what she had heard, and was trying to recall every word that Mr Caldwell had said, in case she forgot some circumstance, however trivial.

Edmund was leaving, Edmund was going away!

If only she had had more time to question Mr Caldwell, or even better, to go and see Mrs Caldwell, she could surely have found out more. He had decided, his father said, suddenly—and on the Saturday, the very day that he had met her, arm in arm with Lord Francis! But was that mere coincidence? Was she refining too much on her impressions? After all, she had no real proof of his affection for her; only that one conversation, that one gesture… it was very natural that a man, an ambitious man, should, on learning of such a bequest, decide on such an adventure.

Barbados! The word had a terrifying ring in her ears. Anne knew very little of the West Indies, but she knew that there were tropical diseases, there were hurricanes, and she was very sure that there were poisonous snakes. He might die before he even arrived there, swept overboard by a storm. If not, he would die of bad food, or be captured by a French privateer, or shot by angry sugar planters for trying to abolish slavery. He would marry a Creole beauty and stay there, and be lost to her for ever. But he was already lost to her—how could she have married him?—when her mother would certainly refuse to meet either him or his parents!

All she could think was that she must get to Burley again; she must find out more. She might say that she wanted to buy more books; she might say she wanted to see her mother again; Lady Catherine had, after all, been very happy to see her, and the visit had been an enjoyable one. Yes! she would do so, she would go there again, as soon as possible. If she were quick, she might even see him; he was going, Mr Caldwell had said, "in a month or so." Oh! how long was that? It could mean almost anything. She would certainly go back to Burley! Perhaps she could persuade Mr Bennet to make the expedition with her, with the promise of spending more time in the fascinating bookstore; after all, she had been so overwhelmed with the hurry of the last few minutes, and the news she had received, that she had not bought one single book!

But this resolution was not carried into effect. The next morning, when Anne was awakened as usual, by her maid, the girl told her that the whole household was in confusion, for Mrs Darcy had been taken ill in the night, four weeks or more before her time, and the month nurse not yet arrived, and nobody dared speak to the master, and Mrs Reynolds was in such a state as never was.

"Mrs Reynolds?" Anne asked. "Why, what has she to do with anything?"

"Well, nothing, miss, as you might say, but there she is, crying and taking on, and it seems she had a sister what died, of a baby, excuse me, miss, and she thinks that Mrs Darcy will die too, because of its being too soon-like."

Anne dressed hurriedly, and went downstairs. There were only Mrs Annesley and Georgiana in the breakfast room, where the meal seemed much less carefully laid than was usual at Pemberley. However, since nobody was eating, this did not seem to be of much moment. Mrs Annesley, looking as composed as usual, told her that, since the month nurse was at a house ten miles away, and was known to have a very sick patient, she would probably not be able to come.

"But Georgiana's old nurse is here," she said. "Since her retirement, she quite often goes to help with the village births, and she is a gentle, clean, sensible creature. Mrs Darcy knows Mrs Grainger well, and likes her so much!" and she smiled at Georgiana, who was looking very white and anxious, and tried in vain to smile back.

The nurse, she said, had already been with Mrs Darcy, and talked ominously of a possible cross-birth, saying that a doctor should be sent for. Mrs Darcy had been seen once by Dr Turley, who was the Lambton practitioner, but she had very much disliked him—had thought him pretentious and vain. Mrs Annesley did not know what to do. She had sent a servant to fetch the two gentlemen, who were walking in the gardens, for, she said, Darcy could neither sit, nor eat, nor speak, and his cousin, not liking to leave him alone, had gone with him.

"Would not Dr Lawson be a better choice?" Anne asked. "He has such good sense, and is so kind; there is no nonsense about him."

At that moment her two cousins entered, and Mrs Annesley repeated the nurse's opinion, and Anne's suggestion to them.

"Lawson!" Darcy said. "He struck me as a sensible fellow. I wish he could be got here. But it is fifteen miles to Burley. It would take a carriage, or even a horse, several hours to cover the distance, and by that time…" and he sat down at the table, and buried his head in his hands.

"Excuse me," said Anne, "but if I recall correctly, cousin, I remember it was mentioned that Mr… Mr Edmund Caldwell's house is but five miles from here, and Mrs Caldwell told me he lived less than half an hour's ride from Burley. I understand that it is not a carriage road, but could the two of you not ride there by that road, and bring Dr Lawson back on horseback? I remember he mentioned that he quite often rides, when he goes to see his patients, for the countryside is so rough."

Darcy looked up. "You are right!" he said. "The track is hilly and steep, it has never been made up for carriage traffic, in bad weather it cannot be used, for so much water comes down— but it cuts off a huge swath of country. Yes, in this weather it will certainly be passable, and we might ride there in an hour, or a little more. Fitzwilliam, will you come with me?"

"Of course," said his cousin. Servants were called, grooms were sent for, all was hurry, bustle, and purpose.

"Stay a moment," Mrs Annesley said. "Hard riding uphill will tire your horses. I will tell the grooms to bring extra horses up, slowly, behind you, and they can meet you as you return. That way you will get back sooner."

"Mrs Annesley, you should be a campaigner," Fitzwilliam exclaimed. "Well thought of, indeed!"

"My husband was a military man," Mrs Annesley said, smiling. "Do you go on your way; I will see to it."

After that, things happened as they will, when gentlemen have made up their minds, and wish to be gone; and within a very short time they were on their way.

"Now," said Mrs Annesley firmly. "I think we should all three sit down, and eat this quite dreadful breakfast. Come, my dears, you must eat something, it will not help Mrs Darcy to have you starve yourselves."

They both tried, but made a poor showing. As they were still at the table, the sound of a horse approaching was heard. Instructions had been given that visitors were to be denied, but the butler entered, and asked if someone would speak briefly with Mr Rackham, who had brought a letter from his mother, which, he said, wanted an answer.

The letter was simple and very kind. Mrs Rackham had heard already, in the mysterious way that everything is known in the country, of Mrs Darcy's situation, and wrote to suggest that Miss Darcy, and if she wished, Miss de Bourgh as well, might like to spend the day with Mary. They would do everything in their power to alleviate the distress of a day as anxious as this one must be, and would send regularly, to ask for any news.

"Oh no!" said Georgiana, faintly. "I cannot leave." But Mrs Annesley thought otherwise. "I shall be very much occupied, my dear Miss Darcy," she said. "The very best thing you can do would be to go. Then I shall have the comfort of knowing that you are in good hands. I assure you, it would help me very much."

Anne was amused to see with what tact Mrs Annesley dealt with Georgiana. As she had already observed, Georgiana was high-strung, and she could see that the prospect of calming her nervous fears, with no idea how long matters might go on, was not an agreeable one. Eventually, Georgiana agreed to go; she would ride in the pony carriage, with Mr Rackham escorting her. "Miss Rackham is one of those people who naturally protect and cherish others," Mrs Annesley observed. "She will look after her friend very well. Now,

Miss de Bourgh, I must go and speak to Mrs Reynolds. The household has rapidly fallen into the sort of disorder that all households do, when unexpected things happen. I think you refused to go to the Rackhams' because you have a purpose; am I right?"

"Yes, indeed," said Anne. "I am going to the library. We have forgotten Mr Bennet. I think I should go to him."

Sure enough, there, in his usual chair, sat Elizabeth's father. He was neither reading, nor writing, and seemed hunched over, as if he had somehow shrunk. Anne had the idea that, if nothing were done, he would sit there all day. Suddenly she wished very much that her mother were there. Lady Catherine would perhaps not understand his misery, or have any sympathy for it, but she would know what to do. She would scold, Anne thought. I cannot. But he is suffering dreadfully; I must do something.

"Mr Bennet!" she said, as firmly and loudly as she could. He looked up, startled.

"Come, sir," she said. "Minette needs her walk, and we need you to come with us. You must, indeed you must," and putting her hand on his arm, she tried to make him get up. The only thing that will get him up, she thought, is if someone needs him. "I cannot go without you, sir. I am alone, and I need you. I am frightened, too."

Whether he were too startled, or too apathetic to resist, she did not know, but he got up; he went with her to the door; the footman was there, with Minette. "Thank you, Thomas," said Anne. She took the dog's leash, guided them both outside, and they went along the terrace, past the formal gardens, until they reached the woodland path that followed the stream.

Chapter 19

THEY SEATED THEMSELVES ON A RUSTIC BENCH, WITH A VIEW OF the beautiful stream and the surrounding countryside. Now that he had a companion, Mr Bennet seemed more at ease, and only wanted to talk, and to talk of Elizabeth. He told Anne of her childhood, of her early promise and childish achievements in talking, in reading, in memory, and what a delightful companion she had proved for him, even as a small girl. Their mother, never averse to expenditure on finery, had thought it not worth the cost of sending them to school. "And indeed, my dear, I think schools for girls do little more than screw the girls out of health and into vanity." He talked of his other daughters, and it was clear to Anne that none of them had the hold on his heart that this child had. It was evident that Jane's outstanding beauty, her mother's pride, seemed insipid to him beside Elizabeth's wit and cleverness; and though Mary shared some of his love of books, he had not thought it worthwhile to cultivate her mind, for she was serious and a little slow. I might get on well with Mary, Anne thought.

Then, to Anne's surprise, he spoke of "Miss Lucas." It was a few moments before Anne realised that he was speaking of Mrs Collins. "I do not know her well," she said, timidly, for she had always avoided entering the Parsonage, whenever the carriage stopped there, disliking Mr Collins' servile and ingratiating ways.

"She is a very brave and sensible woman," Mr Bennet said, abruptly. "Did you know that my Lizzie was supposed to marry that fool, Collins?" Anne did indeed know; she had heard her mother speak on the subject, many times, and ask, why had not the presumptuous Miss Bennet become the parson's wife, and stayed within her station in life, where she belonged?

"But she turned him down, thank God," said her father, "and then poor Miss Lucas turned round, in the twinkling of an eye, and snapped him up. She had not a hope of marriage, but was all set to die an old maid; she may be said to have got him, as they vulgarly say, on the rebound, but she got him. And she has made something of it, that is the remarkable thing. My daughter tells me that she writes with pleasure and enthusiasm of her home, her garden, her occupations, and now her child; and then, too, she has made Collins a happy man, or as happy as such a stupid fellow can be. That, Miss de Bourgh, is what I call courage. We most of us have to make some sort of adjustment to our lot in life; we mostly have to cut our coat to suit the cloth. But for my Lizzie it has not been so; they have found each other, and it is truly a marriage of like minds. He understands her worth. But oh, can you not see, what a ruin, what a desolation it would be, if Elizabeth were lost to us?"

Anne was horrified. She took a deep breath: "Come, sir, there is no need at all to be thinking of such a contingency. Your daughter is a strong, healthy, young woman, this is her first child, and she is receiving the best attention that it is possible to have. Daughters often resemble their mothers in these matters. You have just told me that her mother had five children, and, if I understand you aright, is still in very good health. There is no reason at all for imagining such a thing. There may be some anxiety about the child, but many eight-month, and even seven-month babies live, and do well. Truly, my dear Mr Bennet, I cannot allow you to think of such a thing. Your concern is due to your affection for her, and does you credit, but forgive me, are you not allowing your imagination to run away with you?"

"Well, you may be right. I hope you are right."

"Of course I am right! Come, Minette is trying to chase the squirrels again; come and watch her, foolish little thing."

Back at the house, Mrs Annesley had gone to see Mrs Reynolds, who had somehow convinced herself that both mother and child would die, and was sitting weeping in her room. Mrs Annesley told her firmly to stop crying, for she was needed, and asked her whether anybody had considered that a wet nurse might be wanted.

"Oh no, madam, Mrs Darcy would not think of such a thing, she said she wanted to nurse the child herself—they do nowadays. Lady Anne Darcy always had one, and Lady Catherine too; but times have changed, madam, have they not?"

"Yes, indeed, but I think that it should be thought of, for Mrs Darcy may not be well, things are not just as they ought to be; she may be very exhausted after the child's birth. Tell me, Mrs Reynolds, you know most of the people in Lambton, do you not?"

"Oh, yes, madam, I have lived here all my life."

"Well, I want you to consider, and to ask the other servants as well, whether there is any young woman who could come, for I think someone may be needed."

Mrs Annesley's conviction that mother and child were expected to live, and the thought that she herself was wanted and could be useful, worked powerfully on Mrs Reynolds. She dried her eyes, and set to thinking: She knew of the very person! A young woman living only three miles away, very clean, healthy, "…and she is a Methody, all the family are, and go to the chapel, which I cannot like, but it is all for the best, for they never touch liquor, or even beer." She would at once send to Torgates Farm, and set about making the necessary arrangements; oh yes! the young woman would come if she were needed, anybody would come, to help Pemberley.

Mrs Reynolds' restoration to her usual self quickly restored the spirits of the other servants. "Servants always go to pieces," Mrs Annesley said, "if the person in command is suddenly removed. I told them that Mrs Darcy, when she is up and about again— when, not if—will expect to find that everybody has done their duty, just as if she were there. They are all very fond of her, which helps, and everything was right, once the cook knew what was wanted for dinner, which he could perfectly well have thought of for himself."

Shortly before midday, the gentlemen returned with Dr Lawson. Darcy looked better for his ride, and everyone felt convinced that now things would soon be right. But there was no news, and the afternoon seemed very long. The Rector of the parish came to visit, and was admitted. He was an intelligent, gentlemanly, serious-minded man, to whom Darcy had recently presented the living, saying that he did not want a man who would flatter and obey him, but one who would take care of the people. He sat with them quietly for some time, and then left. Anne did not think that his presence had helped anyone very much, for he was not a man of optimistic mind, and could not hide the fact that he did not know if he would next be called upon to baptize, or to bury.

A little later, Anne proposed that they might attend the evening service, at the church. Mrs Annesley said she would go; Colonel Fitzwilliam wanted to go with them, but did not know whether he should leave Darcy; however, Mr Bennet quietly offered to take Darcy on at a game of chess, or walk with him, whichever he might prefer.

When they got to the church, it was surprisingly full. It seemed that many of the people of Lambton had had the same thought, and as they entered, there was a murmur of quiet sympathy. As they made their way forward to the Darcy pew, Anne saw Georgiana, and with her, Mr Rackham, his mother, and Mary.

The ancient words of the Prayer Book were comforting. Anne felt sorry that it was not the day or time for the Litany, for *one* phrase was certainly in everyone's mind: the words "for all women labouring of child." As they left, people crowded round in silence; some pressed Mrs Annesley's hand. Anne felt glad of their kindness, but understood why Darcy had not wanted to come.

Georgiana returned with them. Dinner was a miserable affair; the cook might as well not have troubled himself, for very little was eaten. When it ended, the gentlemen did not stay behind, but went straight to the drawing room with the ladies. Darcy made for an armchair and sat, his head in his hands.

"I will ring for tea," Mrs Annesley said. "It will do us good. Oh, Forrest, there you are, I was just going to ring…"

But it was not the butler. Dr Lawson stood in the doorway.

"Mr Darcy," he said. Darcy looked up at him. Anne thought, *This is how my cousin will look, when he is old.* "Mr Darcy, sir, you have a son."

Chapter 20

H E IS A FINE YOUNG FELLOW," DR LAWSON SAID. "A LITTLE small, but that was only to be expected; however, there is nothing to worry about, he has every intention of living, and so has his mother. She is sleeping; you may go to her, sir, but you must not speak to her, do not be trying to wake her up. You will have all the time in the world to talk to her, later."

Elizabeth was safe, and she had a son! Anne thought that she had never before experienced such felicity. She and Georgiana threw their arms around each other. She saw tears running down Mr Bennet's face; she thought she saw Colonel Fitzwilliam kiss Mrs Annesley; then she burst into tears herself. Darcy disappeared upstairs. They had recovered their composure somewhat by the time he came down, accompanied by the nurse. She was carrying a swaddled bundle, which contained Lewis Bennet Fitzwilliam Darcy. Her father's name! They had given him her father's name!

Mr Bennet, now quite himself again, looked cautiously at the infant, and observed that he looked very small for such a colossal collection of names. Then Georgiana said, "Oh, my goodness, I am an aunt!" With the child's birth, she had become that happiest and most useful of human beings, an aunt! After the tears, there was laughter; the butler brought wine, and the cook sent up sandwiches and soup, for everybody was suddenly very hungry. Then someone—she thought it was Mrs Annesley—said "Oh, listen!" They all went to the French windows of the drawing room, which were open, for it was a fine, warm night. The church bells were ringing.

The next few days passed in a happy blur of visitors, letters, messages and congratulations. However, they also brought two things to Anne herself that were very welcome. First of all, three new dresses were delivered—three dresses that she had decided on, and ordered, and paid for herself. Hardly had she recovered from the pleasure of trying them on, and finding that she looked delightfully in them, than her cousin came to find her; there was a letter for her.

"It must be from my mother," she thought. But it was not; it was from Mrs Endicott. Mrs Caldwell, it appeared, had read Anne's manuscript to her and her husband, and they were much impressed with it. They both believed that the story, entertaining and lively, would appeal strongly to the public. They hoped very much that Anne would finish the story, and if she were to think of publication, would she do them the favour of discussing the matter with them, before approaching anyone else?

Here was material for delighted reflection! No one else was interested; everyone was busy, everyone was happy; but Anne carried the letter around with her all day, took it out from time to time, and read it again. No letter from a lover is ever more welcome, brings more joy, than a publisher's expression of interest does to a new author! In the midst of her satisfaction, however, Anne had time to wonder: did Edmund know about it? Had he been there, when the story was being read? Had he been the one to read it? Had he thought of her? Was he still at home? The date Mr Caldwell had mentioned was still ahead, but anything could have happened to hasten his journey.

This led to other thoughts: she began reflecting on what Mr Bennet had said to her, while they sat by the stream; that most people have to cut their coat according to their cloth; and that people like Mrs Collins could still have a happy life, or at least, a life of small, quiet satisfactions. He had not said a word about himself, but she suspected, more from what had not been said, that this might be his own situation; and that this was why Elizabeth's marriage was such an especial source of joy to him. Elizabeth, she thought, had taken a great risk in refusing Mr Collins. Her family was not rich, and she might never have got another offer of marriage. As it turned out, she had been right; but what a risk she had taken!

But what did all this mean for her? What bearing did it have on her own situation? Ought she, like Mrs Collins, to find a suitable, good-natured husband, and make what she could of a less rapturous, but possibly quite happy marriage? Ought she to forget her love? Forget Edmund? Never! She could think of no one among her circle of acquaintances who might replace Edmund in her heart. No! she could not do it; like Elizabeth, she could not make do with someone else. There was to be no second-best for her.

But since he could not marry her? Well, possibly friendship could take the place of love. When he came back, or if he came back, he would have forgotten her, and would marry someone else (if he did not bring back the Creole beauty); and sitting alone, thinking along these melancholy lines, she had been present at his wedding, stood godmother to several of his children, and would shortly have attended his funeral, had not Georgiana come to the library to call her to go riding.

Pretty soon, however, all these reflections were thrust into the background, for Lady Catherine came to Pemberley.

She was just as cheerful as she had been at Burley: just as smiling, just as fashionably clad. Anne had never seen her so much the great lady; her very hat gave out intimations of splendour. She patted Georgiana's cheek, and remarked that she had been much admired at the ball; she was civil to Mr Bennet, and even Mrs Annesley got two fingers, and a gracious nod. Although visitors were not yet allowed into Elizabeth's bedroom, she must of course be admitted; and the experience was very satisfactory, for she observed at once that young Lewis Bennet Fitzwilliam was occupying the magnificent cradle that had been a gift to Lady Anne Darcy from her father, Lord Waterson. To Elizabeth, she was extremely gracious; there was little to say once the infant had been admired, and his astonishing resemblance to her late father remarked upon (which resemblance might be said to consist in the fact that each had a nose, and two eyes), and she had the good sense, which more affectionate visitors often lack, to bring her visit to a rapid conclusion. She emerged from the visit smiling cheerfully.

The reason was soon to become apparent; she had lost nothing; she was no longer interested in the reversion of Pemberley. As soon as she had left Elizabeth's bedchamber, she requested a private interview with her daughter. Anne took her to a small salon, seldom used.

"My dear Anne, I am very happy to see you still looking so remarkably well," her mother said. "The Duchess complimented me on your looks only yesterday. I would never have thought that your health could have improved so much. The air of Pemberley agrees with you, it seems."

"It does, indeed, madam."

"Well, it could not have happened at a better time, for now I have something to tell you that will do you more good still. I am happy to felicitate you on your approaching marriage. Lord Francis Meaburn has requested my permission to pay his addresses to you. I need hardly tell you with what happiness I have given my consent."

"Lord Francis?" said Anne, stupidly. "But he… but I…"

"What?"

"I… I had no idea that he… it cannot be. I have had only the briefest of conversations with him. There must be some mistake."

"On the contrary, there is no mistake. The Duchess tells me that he is very much taken with you."

"And what did he say?"

"He? Nothing. His sister has arranged it all, with his agreement, and I may say, you are in high luck to meet with the approval of such a family. Their rank is lofty, and their connections—"

"One moment, madam, I pray you," said Anne. "The matter is not so simple. If rank were all that were needed in a husband, I might have no objection. His father is a Duke, and his brother is a Duke, and they are all Dukes together. But I do not want a Duke. I want a husband, and I would like one who began by doing his proposing for himself, and who would propose to me, not to my mother."

"Really, Anne! There is no occasion to speak in such a disrespectful manner! Lord Francis has behaved very correctly."

"Then I will refuse him with equal correctness. I have walked with him once and danced with him twice. I did not like him, and I am not minded to marry him."

"I agree, it is a little sudden. Had things been otherwise, I would not have acceded to this proposal at this time. I was waiting to be sure that a more splendid position was not open to you; in other words, had matters here turned out as they might well have done, I would have been the first to urge you to stay here, and wait for a few months, to see how matters turned out then."

"I do not understand."

"As it happens, things have gone well, your cousin has an heir, and his wife is safe. While not *wishing* for a different outcome, it was only prudent to be prepared for it; a man of his standing, should he lose his wife, must marry again, and soon: he has his inheritance to think of, and he is not getting any younger. Had things transpired that way, I think there is little doubt that you would have been the next mistress of Pemberley; for he would not be likely to look further for a second wife, than a cousin, living already in the house, known and liked by him. But all that is at an end, not to be thought of."

Anne could hardly believe her ears. Her mother had actually been—no, not scheming, not even wishing for—but certainly, as in the vulgar phrase, hedging her bets, on the terrible possibility of Elizabeth's death! That anyone should think of such a melancholy and shocking extremity as something to be anticipated, seemed to her so horrifying that she could hardly believe that she was hearing it. But it was so; her mother had said it.

"I cannot believe, madam, for one moment, that you were hoping for such a terrible eventuality."

"Of course not, that would be very wrong; but why else should we set forth for Pemberley, at the time we did? Come, Anne, do not be so nice, is not the position of mistress of Pemberley one that is worth struggling, conspiring, even fighting for? Would it not have been worth it, had you been here at the right time?"

"No! No! I cannot even think of such a terrible possibility. As for Lord Francis, ma'am, if he will come here, I will consider

him, I will listen to what he has to say, but I must warn you…
I am sure he is very good-natured, but it needs more than that
to make a marriage. There… there must be, if not love, at least
affection and respect, and I think there should be some community of interest. He is a man of fashion; my interests are centered
in a quiet life in the country. I am not beautiful, I am not lively,
I should be very unhappy in a fashionable drawing room. I love
to write; do you think Lord Francis wants a wife who is writing
a book?"

"Writing a book? Why, what nonsense is this? Do you mean—a
novel? Do you intend to publish such a thing? to put our family
name on the cover of a vulgar work of fiction, like some parson's
daughter who is glad to make twenty pounds, or thirty, out of
publishing her work?"

Anne's heart was hammering against her ribs, but she must not
give up; she must not give in to her mother.

"Setting that aside for the moment, I am not a parson's daughter,
I am your daughter, madam. Would you allow others to tell you to
marry a man whom you did not want to marry?"

Lady Catherine was not a loving mother, but she was not an
unnatural one, either. She genuinely believed that, by encouraging
Anne to this marriage, she was promoting Anne's best interests and
doing what would make her happy; most people think that what
is good for them must be right for others, and at Anne's age, such
a marriage would have made *Lady Catherine* very happy. With her
improved health had come an improvement in temper, and she had
no intention of alarming or distressing her daughter. But she could
not understand. "Why? What is this? How comes this about? You
have barely met him, and yet you are sure that you do not want to
marry him? How is this possible?"

"It is very simple, madam; I believe his only reason in wanting to marry me is his lack of money. I have money, but he has nothing to offer *me* except his rank. You are interested in rank; I am not."

Lady Catherine had every wish to be affectionate, to be conciliating; but this was too much for her. "So! Are you one of these people who wish to overturn the way our world is run? Do you wish to do away with all the distinctions of rank, and have every plough man the equal of a lord? Unhappy girl! You are being offered a position that anyone in the kingdom might envy. We have never been ennobled; the Stilbury connection would put all of us at the centre of influence and power. Do you realize what it might mean for your family? for Darcy's boy? for any children you might have? And you turn this down, on a whim? Is this some theory that your stonemason has taught you? Do you still cherish the desire to lower yourself by associating with such people?"

As she spoke, Lady Catherine rose from her seat, and stood over Anne. Anne tried to rise, but as she did so, Minette, sensing Anne's distress, began barking and growling, clearly terrified, backing and showing her teeth. Anne stood up, turned away, caught her skirts in the little dog's leash, tried to right herself, fell, and knew no more.

Chapter 21

Lady Catherine felt no inclination to blame herself on seeing her daughter unconscious on the floor; after all, the accident was caused by that ridiculous little dog: it was not *her* fault. She did as much as she felt any mother ought to do by ringing the bell, and sending the butler for help; and she would undoubtedly have dashed a glass of water onto Anne's face, if such a thing had been available. In spite of these attentions, it was known to every servant in Pemberley—house, gardens, and stables—in the space of a quarter of an hour, that Miss de Bourgh was dead, and that her mother had murdered her. It was even the subject of speculation whether she would be hanged, or whether, as some opined, being such a great lady, they could never stick it to her in a trial.

Anne recovered consciousness almost at once, and found that her mother was nowhere in sight, but that her maid, Georgiana's maid, Georgiana, the housekeeper, and Mrs Annesley were all hovering over her, and trying to attend to her. She declared that she was well, very well, so foolish of her! Nothing had happened, she had tripped; there was nothing the matter, only a slight bump on her head. However, when she tried to walk, she felt so faint and dizzy that she was obliged to sit down at once, and Mrs Annesley had no hesitation in directing that she was to be taken upstairs, and put to bed. "But Minette; let me take Minette with me."

"No, my dear," said Mrs Annesley. "Minette must stay; see, Miss Darcy will look after her, will you not, Miss Darcy?"

"Of course," said Georgiana.

"No, no," said poor Anne. "Someone may hurt her; it was not her fault," and nothing would persuade her that the dog was safe with them. She became so agitated that, in the end, Mrs Annesley, who was pretty sure that Anne had a concussion, and that she should be kept quiet, herself carried Minette up to her bedchamber.

Meanwhile it fell to her cousin Darcy's lot to deal with Lady Catherine. As they paced the terrace and entered the formal gardens, his aunt made the full situation pretty clear. While not knowing precisely what had happened, he understood that Anne had received an offer of marriage, that there had been some kind of altercation, which did not surprise him in the least, and that in spite of her wish to be ingratiating, his aunt's temper had got the better of her. She was angry, but even more she was surprised.

"Such a marriage as she could never have dreamed of! For even now, and I must say her looks have much improved, she is not remarkably *au fait de beaute,* but the Duchess is very much impressed with her, and so is he; and you know, nephew, he could look for a wife in the highest circles in the land. I am very much shocked, I am very much disappointed. Think what it could mean to the whole family, to your son, when he is grown, to have relatives in such a lofty position!"

"That is possibly true, but I do not think it would much gratify Lewis or myself to have his elevation due to his cousin's marriage, rather than to his own character and efforts."

"Nonsense! Everybody utilizes their family connections to their advantage, it is the way things are done—families rise or fall together. The gravel on these paths is very coarse; we use a finer one, at Rosings."

"This gravel dries better, when it has been raining."

"When it rains, *we* stay indoors. And I wish to know, for one thing, who has been encouraging Anne in these revolutionary opinions she seems to have adopted. For I am sure that she has not learned them from you?"

"Certainly not."

"She reads too much; that is what has done the damage. By the way, that topiary, how often do you have it cut back?"

"About every six weeks."

"If you get them to do it once a month, you will get a better result. No, I am very disappointed. If you had some other suitor to propose…"

Darcy mentioned Sir Matthew, Mr Granby, and Mr Kirkman, but in vain; his aunt was clearly familiar with the old saying about the "bird in the hand."

"Yes, but that is not the same as an offer, a direct offer of marriage. Their attentions may mean nothing—and as for taking this Mr Kirkman, an elderly widower, with no title, instead of Lord Francis Meaburn! Certainly not!"

"Dare I mention, aunt, that Lord Francis is a widower, and by no means young?"

"Nonsense, he is hardly more than forty. Your father brought that marble figure from Italy; we have a far finer one at Rosings. You would do well to cut back those laurels; you would get a better view of it from the wilderness."

"I think there is one thing I must make clear to you, ma'am: my cousin is five-and-twenty years old, and she knows her own mind.

She dislikes Lord Francis, as she has made abundantly clear; and for my part, given the differences between them, I cannot believe that it would be a happy marriage."

"Pooh! Nonsense; he is as good-natured a man as ever lived. There is no reason why he would not make a perfectly amiable husband. If she is so foolish as to wish to write books, he is not likely to raise any objection."

"No, as long as he has money to spend on his gambling and profligacies. I am surprised, ma'am, that you would wish to see the resources you have husbanded so well, at risk of being wasted."

"Oh! He has given up his gambling; all that is at an end. Of course Anne's money would be tied up, in some way. The lawyers would see to it. In any case, she cannot stay here for the rest of her life. Well! She must come back to Rosings with me. We will have the Duchess and her brother down to visit, for she has several times said that she would like to see the place, and we will see if Anne cannot be persuaded. But she is not to bring that detestable little dog with her; I cannot abide it. It is savage, and should be shot."

"I beg you, madam, do not attempt to persuade her into an unhappy marriage."

"You married to please yourself, and it has turned out well; now you think that every marriage, made for family reasons rather than love, must be unhappy. It is not so. And Anne is not the girl to choose well, left to herself. Stay—she has not done so? Is *that* the reason for all this high-flown sentiment? Has she said anything to lead you to think that she has some person in mind?"

"No, madam."

"Then answer me: who gave her the dog?"

"I could not lie to her," Darcy told his wife, later. "I made it clear that Caldwell had abandoned all pretension to her hand, and is leaving the country besides, and that she has said nothing as to any attachment; but I could not lie."

And Lady Catherine marched back to the house to speak to her daughter. When she went to climb the stairs, however, she found herself confronted by Dr Lawson. He had ridden over to take a look at Mrs Darcy, and found that she was very well. But Anne was a different matter. He remembered Lady Catherine, and waited for no greeting.

"If you are thinking of seeing your daughter, madam," he said, "it is impossible; you must wait."

"Must? Must? Nonsense, man! It cannot hurt her to see her mother. Stand aside."

Dr Lawson was a large man, and his bulk effectively blocked the stairway. He did not budge.

"Do you want to kill her, madam?"

"Out of my way, sir!"

Dr Lawson repeated, "Do you want to kill her, madam? She has had a severe concussion; she is sleeping; she must not be disturbed."

"Oh, very well. But I cannot be hanging about here all day, I wish to be on my way. I will write to her. Darcy, I must ask you for the use of your writing desk."

"Very well, ma'am. But my cousin is not well. I beg you not to write what will distress her."

"I think, nephew, a mother is the best judge of what she may write to her daughter." And Lady Catherine sat down to write.

When Anne read the letter, it threw her into a fever. Her worst terror was the threat to Minette. She could even bear to go back to Rosings, she thought, but she would rather die than go there and risk her dog's life. No, she did not trust anyone. Her mother might promise to spare Minette, but then if she so much as growled at some servant or keeper, there would be the excuse to get rid of her. If Minette died, she would die, too. Or, if worst came to worst, rather than die, she would marry Lord Francis, at least he had said that he liked the dog—but would she be able to keep Minette alive until the wedding day? Perhaps she could leave Minette at Pemberley for a while—but the idea threw her into a passion of tears. Dr Lawson became anxious.

Chapter 22

ANNE WAS ILL WITH MISERY ALL THAT DAY AND THE NEXT. THEN something strange happened. At some time, in the middle of a sleepless night, she began, instead of suffering, to think. It was not good enough to cry; crying would not save her or Minette; she must do something. It was never of any use to appeal to her mother's sympathy—she never felt sorry for anyone. Nor was maternal affection a powerful impulse with her. She got her way by being forceful, by being determined, by always being sure that she was right. Well! She was her mother's daughter; she would use her mother's weapons; supposing *her* to be in this situation, what would Lady Catherine do?

She could not refuse to go to Rosings; no young woman could do such a thing; it was beyond the bounds of possibility. Nor could she ask her cousins at Pemberley to house her in defiance of her mother's expressed wish; such a request would place them in a position of great embarrassment. However, suppose she could make it clear to Lady Catherine that she was a different person now, that living at Rosings would be a different experience for both of them?

As soon as it was light, Anne rang for her maid, got herself put into a dressing gown, and writing materials brought, and wrote a letter. It took her several hours, and we will not enquire how many sheets were left torn up on the floor, but the letter was eventually written:

Madam,

The respect due to a parent makes it impossible for me to propose disobeying your commands; but I do request you to reflect. You wish me to come to Rosings with you, and I have no intention of refusing, although because of the injury to my head, it will not be possible for me to travel, probably for many weeks.

You wish me to accept Lord Francis's offer of marriage, and out of respect for your wishes, I will re-consider his offer, but only when he comes to me, and makes it himself. He can do so, if he wishes, more expeditiously from Burley, than by going into Kent. That is, I will consider it—I do not say that I will accept it. My wealth and rank have, as you know, prevented my thinking of marriage with a man with whom I believe I could have been happy. Wealth and rank are not going to force me into marrying a man whom I do not love, and who does not love me.

You wish me to reside with you at Rosings: you have yourself acknowledged that my improvement in health dates from my leaving Rosings. The location does not agree with me, I have never been well there, and I do not wish to return to a state of sickness. If, in deference to your wishes, I must reside there, I will not have Dr Fillgrave as my medical advisor. I will choose my own doctor, and pay him myself. I must have a horse to ride.

I must have a personal maid-companion of my own; I will not be attended by Mullins. Above all, I will not be carried here and there to seek a husband; I shall spend my time in the library, writing. I intend to publish my writing; however, in deference to your views, I will publish under a pseudonym.

I think we are both agreed that it is high time for me to find an establishment in life, but are disagreed on what that establishment should be. I am of full age and know what I want. I require a similarity of interests; I require a situation of mutual respect and affection; and if such a situation is not available, I am resigned to spending the rest of my life as an unmarried woman. We left Rosings because there were no prospects of marriage for me in such a restricted society. I believe my chances of finding the establishment I need are far better here than at Rosings, and this is where I wish to remain. I beg you, madam, to return to Rosings and leave me here.

As for the dog, she is not dangerous, and I will not allow her to be destroyed. She has never bitten or snapped, and did not do so yesterday; raised voices frighten her and she growled and barked, that is all. I will not come to Rosings, or go anywhere else, without her, and she will never leave my side. If you refuse to allow her to enter your drawing-room, I will not enter it, either.

Believe me, madam,
Yours very sincerely,

Anne de Bourgh

As soon as the letter was written, Anne had breakfast brought to her. Then she decided to try to get dressed. She found to her surprise that she had much more strength than she had expected. To all enquiries, she caused the reply to be given that "she was better, and would be downstairs shortly."

About mid-morning she went downstairs, saw to the letter's being dispatched, and herself walked Minette. Then she went to the drawing room. There was a visitor there, Lady Louisa. And more than that: her cousin Elizabeth was there, as well. She had made a rapid recovery, due, Dr Lawson said, to her youth, a good constitution, and happiness. Mrs Grainger's predictions had not been realized, the obliging young woman from Torgates had not been needed, and a very few days after her child's birth, Mrs Darcy had announced that she was tired to death with her bedchamber, and did not wish to stay there. Sitting on the sofa, with her baby in her arms, she looked more lovely than Anne had ever seen her.

A conference had been going on, and she was its subject. The unknown, disregarded cousin had become a loved and valued citizen of Pemberley; she who had been thought of as a burden was now an asset; and everyone was there, including Mr Bennet, to discuss her situation, and what they might do to help her. Lady Louisa had arrived with a scheme of her own, but heard it all out in her usual alert, kindly manner, saying nothing until everyone had spoken, and she had the full history of Lady Catherine's visit.

Mr Darcy had alluded—as he thought, very delicately—to the subject of Lady Catherine's disagreement with Anne, but Lady Louisa had no time for delicacy.

"In love with somebody else, is she?" she said. "Well, I am not surprised, it always happens so with your lonely, cloistered girls, who cannot tell anybody about their feelings, and keep things to themselves. Give me a girl who cries, and writes love-letters, and keeps her sisters awake at night; she will grow out of it. Miss de Bourgh has been kept too close, had nobody to confide in; girls like her always fall in love with the first man who is kind to them, and never get over it. And her family can think themselves lucky if it's not a dancing-master, or a groom of the chambers, or some such thing."

There was a kind of sudden stillness in the room, and Lady Louisa saw that Georgiana's face was scarlet. *So... there was something!* she thought. *I'll wager fifty sovereigns, it was that handsome scamp, what was his name, Wigby or Wilson—the steward's son. It seems to run in the family.* "Now, what is to be done?"

It was at this point, fortunately, that Anne entered the room. There was a general expression of delight on seeing her, and in the middle of the exclamations, and enquiries as to her health, and finding her a comfortable chair, and Anne being allowed to take little Lewis in her arms and admire him, Georgiana's complexion had a chance to recover.

However, at this point, there was another interruption. Mr Lewis Bennet Fitzwilliam Darcy, having been disturbed, and picked up, and kissed, chose this moment to demand attentions from his mother that only she could provide; and Elizabeth was obliged to leave them. "But," she said, "you have matters well in hand, and you have my full approbation for whatever you may decide, and any assistance that Lewis and I can give."

As soon as they were all settled, Lady Louisa brought up the reason why she had come to Pemberley; she was going to London in a few weeks, and wished to invite Georgiana to go with her, and have a season in town. She was of the opinion that Georgiana needed the society of more young people, "and not young men," she said, "so much as young girls; she needs to spend more time with young women of her own age. Look how happy she is when she is with Miss Rackham. You need to laugh with other girls, Georgiana, to be foolish if you will; you need to be young."

"You are right," said Darcy. "She must leave us old married people to themselves."

"Well, I see no reason why Miss de Bourgh, if she is well enough by then, should not come too," Lady Louisa said. "It would be far better for you, my dear, than going back to Rosings; yes, yes, Minette would be welcome. If she comes to London," she pointed out, "Miss de Bourgh will certainly meet Lord Francis, for he is sure to be there for the season; but she will also meet other eligible gentlemen. After all, with thirty thousand pounds, why should the heiress of Rosings be limited to considering one elderly suitor, whom she does not like? She might do far better."

"But supposing Lady Catherine decides to go to London?" Mr Bennet asked.

"She will not do so," said Lady Louisa. "I have known her for five-and-thirty years, and she will never go anywhere that she is not first in importance. That is why she has been so happy at Rosings, where she rules; that is why she likes Burley, where she is outdone only by the Duchess, who treats her as an equal because she hopes for a rich wife for her brother. She will not go to London. But she may well let Miss de Bourgh go; believe me, she sincerely desires what is best for her daughter."

Anne could only listen, and thank her, and hope.

On this basis, a plan was concocted. Lady Louisa's ball was to take place within a few days; everyone should go, except Anne. Mrs Darcy, of course, was not able to go, and Mr Bennet, who did not like balls, would stay to bear them company. They should all insist to Lady Catherine that Anne was really unwell, and must stay for the time being at Pemberley. At the ball, or more probably the next day (for they must stay the night), they would mention the plan of Georgiana's going to London. Lady Catherine, it was felt, would certainly approve of Georgiana's having a London season, since it would materially increase her chances of getting an eligible husband. Georgiana would then beg as a favour that Anne should join her and Lady Louisa for the season, and Lady Louisa would put forward every argument in her power to persuade Lady Catherine of the eligibility of the plan.

"I am sorry," Mr Bennet said, "to be of so little use to Miss de Bourgh that I can only assist her by *not* being present, but it is just as well. I have had letters from home, and I must leave you all pretty soon. My new granddaughter, little Miss Bingley, is to be christened next week, and they seem to think the child cannot become a Christian unless I am there to witness the proceedings."

There were exclamations of regret, but everyone must acknowledge that it was, indeed, time for him to rejoin his wife and daughters. In addition, he would be able to describe in person all the perfections of little Lewis, "but nobody shall make plans for their marriage," Darcy said. "Look what a bad thing it is, to decide these matters on behalf of two people, while they are still in the cradle."

"I have something to tell you, too," said Colonel Fitzwilliam, "and perhaps it might be as well not to mention this to Lady Catherine, as we do not want to make her angry. I have been recalled. I must return to my regiment in a very few days; and I find that I do not like the idea of being parted from Mrs Annesley. So I have asked her to marry me, and she has said yes. She has been a soldier's wife before and likes the idea of being one again. We plan to marry very quietly, a couple of days after the ball, and we will leave together immediately after the ceremony."

There was no one who was not surprised on hearing the news; there was no one who was not delighted. But as for marrying quietly! They were not to think of it, for everyone wished to be there, and as for leaving right after! No! No! there must be a breakfast. Mrs Annesley hastily explained that "quietly" of course meant "only their friends," and "immediately after" meant "after the breakfast." In response to a discreet question from Darcy, Colonel Fitzwilliam explained in an undertone that his godfather, who had recently died, had left him a sum of money quite sufficient, with care and good sense, to support the expense of a family.

Anne could only be happy for them, though when she was alone, it must be a subject for melancholy reflection, to contrast their happiness, and perfect suitability for each other, with her own situation. She grudged them nothing; she could only long for such felicity for herself, and fear that it was not to be.

Chapter 23

A NNE ENJOYED DANCING NOW, SO MUCH THAT SHE WAS VERY sorry not to go to Lady Louisa's ball; but it could not be. Her head was still tender, and the very thought of an evening of noise, activity, and music made her feel ill. In any case, her mother was hardly likely to believe her still unwell, if she were there. She saw the others on their way, and spent a quiet afternoon and evening with Elizabeth and her father. The dancing party would not return until the next day.

She awaited their return with some confidence. Given their activities and her own letter, she thought her mother might be quite happy to renounce her company at Rosings, and see what London could do for her. What it could do, she was not quite certain; but at least, it would offer her more choices, more possibilities, than life at Rosings. In London, Lady Louisa said, there were groups of people who loved the world of letters; perhaps, among them, she would find a congenial marriage. At the very least, Lord Francis might very likely marry somebody else by the time the season was over.

But all these conjectures were wasted. When they returned the next day, Georgiana almost tumbled out of the carriage, in her haste to tell the news: "Lady Catherine was not at the ball! Neither was the Duchess, nor Lord Francis. No one can imagine what has happened. For the whole of the early part of the evening, they were expected, and with every carriage that was heard to draw up, the news flew round the room, and everyone said 'They have arrived!' But it was not so; they never came."

What had happened? Had some sickness laid them all low? Speculation had run high amongst those attending, Georgiana said, but nobody knew anything, and at last everyone forgot about them, and fell to enjoying themselves. "My brother and the Colonel have ridden into Burley to make enquiries; so we shall soon know more." But Darcy and the Colonel returned, and all that they had discovered was that all three had gone; they had left Burley the previous day. No messages had been left; no letter was received at Pemberley; they seemed to have vanished into thin air.

Well! at least, her mother was not about to descend, as Anne had occasionally feared, and require her to jump into the carriage, and be carried away to Rosings. Presumably her mother had gone back thither. "Surely she has!" said Elizabeth, "for there certainly must be matters to attend to, farms to visit, tenants to be scolded, after an interval of so many weeks. Think of the number of people who need new shelves in their closets!"

Undoubtedly they would hear from her in due course, but for now the whole matter was forgotten, as the time rapidly approached for the marriage of Mrs Annesley and Colonel Fitzwilliam. There was no making of bride-clothes, there were no lace veils or bevy of bridesmaids, no display of costly gifts. A special licence having, by Darcy's activity, been obtained, they all went down to the church in the early morning, and the marriage took place at the conclusion of the morning service. How quiet the ceremony was! And how significant! For the first time, Anne observed the fact that, in this most important of ceremonies, only Christian names are used; it matters not whether the groom be an Earl, or the bride, a princess: John marries Mary. Reflecting on it, she found herself thinking—she must think—*why could I not marry him; what does rank matter?* But in the everyday business of life, she knew, it did.

Mr Bennet left with the married couple, to share the first part of their journey, until their ways should divide.

Their society was now much restricted, and life at Pemberley became very quiet, but it was a busy, happy quiet. A new master was found, to give Anne her piano lessons; and her riding had improved so much that Georgiana, and the groom, were the only companions she needed. The English summer followed its usual pattern, and a spell of bad weather set in, with rain and cold. It sent Anne to the library, to work steadily on her book. She read it aloud, every evening, and it was almost concluded. None of the Darcys saw any reason why she should not publish it, and various absurd pseudonyms were, at one time or another, suggested.

Then there was an assembly at Lambton, at which Anne, wearing the bronze-green silk, danced almost every dance. Sir Matthew danced with her twice.

A few days later, his mother, together with her younger daughter, Miss Zara Brocklebank, visited Pemberley and, while the girls were strolling about the gardens, had a quiet discussion with Mr Darcy as to Anne's exact prospects. "She did it very well, and one cannot blame them," Darcy said. "The family has no money, and he must marry well as to fortune. He is a pleasant fellow, and if you liked him, cousin, you could do much worse. Truly, we will not urge you. But I thought it right to drop you a hint, so that you may think it over, and know your own mind."

Anne thought about it. The date set for the departure of Edmund must have passed; although she had heard nothing, she must assume that he was gone. Even as a beloved guest at Pemberley, she was heartily tired of her single state, which reduced her to the status of a girl, though she was a woman grown. Marriage with Sir Matthew would in many ways be entirely suitable. He was very good-natured; he would be a good steward of Rosings, making few demands for money, as long as he had his horses and his hunting, which the estate could well provide. His rank, his good looks, and his youth would make him acceptable to her mother; and he would not antagonize Lady Catherine with his opinions, for he had none. Alas, Anne could only recall the wedding service she had so recently attended, and "the mutual society, help, and comfort the one should have of the other" would not go out of her mind. It would be a marriage with a man with whom she hardly shared a thought; she could not contemplate it.

Little Lewis continued to thrive, and it was now almost certain that the entire Bennet family, as well as the Bingleys, would come north for the child's christening, in a few weeks, as soon as Mrs Bingley was considered well enough to travel. The question being urgently canvassed by the family was, what should be done about the Bennet sister known as "Lydia." Should she be invited? Would it be possible to invite her, and not include her husband? Anne felt she would quite like to meet the obviously fascinating Mr Wickham. Surely his eloping with Lydia should be overlooked? They were, after all, married now. But there was something unsaid, some other reason why he was not an acceptable visitor at Pemberley, and it was clear in any case that Lydia herself was not much liked. Elizabeth described her as noisy, silly, and indiscreet, and said that Darcy disliked her almost as much as her husband.

One morning, while they were all having breakfast, Darcy was reading the newspaper. Suddenly he exclaimed "Good G——!" and carelessly setting down his cup, spilt coffee all over the table.

"Whatever is it, my love?" his wife asked.

"When gentlemen are reading the newspaper," she said to Anne, "expletives are to be expected, but usually it is only some promotion at the Admiralty or some squabble at a Ministry, or some such thing. When it comes to spilling coffee, it is rather more serious. What is it, my love?" but Darcy seemed almost unable to speak.

"She has married him! She has married him!" was all that he could say; and crushing the paper together, he said to his wife, "It concerns Anne; I do not know how to tell her; we should speak together alone."

"Come, my dear," Elizabeth said. "Anne is not a child; she can hear it, whatever it is."

"Indeed I can," Anne said. "Come, cousin, who has married whom? I hope," she added, laughing, "that it is Lord Francis, then I should be rid of him."

"It is indeed Lord Francis," Darcy said, "but he has married…"

"Well?"

"He has married your mother."

There it was, in all the awful certainty of print, and all the clarity of black and white: *On the —th, at Stilbury Castle, in a private ceremony, the Lady Catherine, relict of Sir Lewis de Bourgh, to Lord Francis Meaburn, second son of the Duke of H——.*

Lady Catherine had married Lord Francis Meaburn.

Chapter 24

THE NEWS STRUCK THEM SPEECHLESS. THE AWESOME LADY Catherine was a widow no more! Come to that, she was "Lady Catherine" no more; and indeed, for the first few startled moments, Anne wondered if she were still her mother.

This was the reason for her disappearance! this the reason for her silence! Once they could speak, everyone had a question, everyone had a conjecture. Elizabeth wondered whose idea the match had been; it must, she thought, be the Duchess who had thought of it. Darcy wanted to know what kind of bargain Lord Francis had driven: "My aunt talked of money being tied up," he said, "but it is not so easy to tie up the income of a married woman, who is unlikely to have any children." Georgiana wondered how two such old people could get married.

"How old are they?" Elizabeth asked.

"I do not think that there is so great a disparity," Darcy said. "I found out the other day, when we thought he might marry Anne—I looked him up in the Peerage—that Lord Francis is three-and-forty, and I believe my aunt is not yet fifty."

"She is eight-and-forty," Anne said. "She is closer in age to him than I am, though of course she is older, not younger."

What could have driven them to such a match? "I think the reason is obvious," Darcy said. "On his side, money; he needs money very badly. On her side, rank; she has become the sister of a Duchess and, since Meaburn's father is still alive, the daughter of a Duke. She will stay at Stilbury—indeed, clearly, she is already there. She will visit at Deepcombe, the Meaburn estate."

"But how will she like it, associating with such great people?" Elizabeth asked. "She will not be able to scold and manage them, as she does her tenants at Rosings."

"Could she get a post at the court?" Georgiana asked.

"I imagine so," said her brother, "if she wished it, and would be happy to stand, wearing all her diamonds, in silence, for three hours together."

"Might she be a Duchess, one day?"

"No," said Darcy. "There are two older brothers, each with several children. A half-dozen people would have to die before she became a Duchess."

Elizabeth caught her breath on the observation that things often turned out the way Lady Catherine wanted them to, and only thought to herself that she would not wager a great deal of money on the lives of the little Meaburns.

At that moment, the butler entered. "Excuse me, madam, sir, the post has arrived, and there is a packet of letters for Mr Darcy, which must be paid for, and will be quite costly, but I do not know the sender. Should it be returned, or do you know a person named Lady Francis Meaburn?"

"No, I do not…" Darcy began. "Yes, of course I do. Yes, Forrest, yes! Pay; and bring it here as fast as you can. It is my aunt! That is her married name!"

The packet was brought, and was almost torn open in the hurry of everyone to satisfy their curiosity. Clearly, it should have been delivered earlier, but the newspaper had arrived first. It might be some vagary of the post office. "But I wonder if they waited, in the hope of getting a frank," Darcy said. "I think that the Duke of Stilbury is seldom at home. They may have waited a day or so, and then sent it."

There were two letters, one for Darcy, and one for Anne, and two legal-looking documents, which turned out to be a copy of Lady Catherine's marriage lines, and a copy of Sir Lewis de Bourgh's Will. "*That* was what they were waiting for," said Darcy. "Colby must have had to hurry from Rosings to Stilbury with it."

The sum of the letters was that, "according to established usage," Lady Catherine's entire assets had been made over to her new husband, as it would all be needed to keep the newly married couple in their station in life. This meant that no provision would in future be made for Anne, "in view of her recalcitrance in the matter of a suitable marriage," beyond the income she was already receiving from the estate of Sir Lewis de Bourgh. Further, she should not expect the property known as Rosings Park, in Kent, to be bequeathed to her, for, as the Will clearly showed, it was the unentailed property of her mother.

"Established usage, indeed?" said Darcy, "to deprive a daughter of her entire dowry? Lord Francis has driven a hard bargain."

"More probably his sister," Elizabeth said.

"However," her mother's letter informed Anne:

> In order to create a proper provision for you, the Duchess has a cousin, the Reverend and Honourable Septimus Whiley, who is willing to marry you. Upon

your acceptance, a provision of ten thousand pounds will be made for you. He is currently the incumbent of Munge Parva, near Stilbury Castle, with a stipend of six hundred pounds a year. He should be a highly suitable husband for you, as his tastes are literary and his habits scholarly. He has been for the past ten years engaged on a learned commentary on the Epistle to the Galatians, and will be glad to have an amanuensis to copy out his manuscript in a fair hand, and prepare an Index.

In addition, on the demise of Mr Bennet, Mr and Mrs Collins will vacate the living of Hunsford, by previous arrangement with me, and remove to Longbourn. At that time I shall present the living to Mr Whiley, and you will remove to Hunsford Parsonage, and live near, though not at, Rosings.

"Oh, he sounds dreadful!" Georgiana cried. "Anne, you must not marry him! Brother, tell her she must not!"

But Darcy appeared to be in a brown study. "What?" he said, after a moment. "No, of course she must not, that is, no, nothing must be done."

"I will not!" Anne exclaimed. "No one shall tell me whom to marry, ever again. I shall live by myself, and write books. Cousin, will you rent the little White Cottage to me, and let me live there?"

"Certainly not," said her cousin. "My dear"—turning to his wife—"I must go out. I forgot, I have not put on riding clothes; I must change, for I have business."

"But it rains."

"Only a little, and it will clear up."

"Will you not go in the carriage?"

"No, it would not do. I must speak to you before I leave, come with me but one moment," and grasping his wife's hand, he almost dragged her out of the room.

Anne and Georgiana were left to look at one another in stupefaction. "But, Anne," Georgiana almost whispered, "she is your mother." This was the thought that had been in Anne's mind since she had heard the news, this was the realization that gave her pain: that a mother should forget, should ignore her feelings for a daughter so far as to marry, to take on new responsibilities, new duties, and even to have the name of de Bourgh subsumed into a new one, without any discussion, any warning, even!

But as she thought of it, it seemed very much in her mother's character: that decided, impulsive nature; that high opinion of her prestige and powers that believed she could not be wrong; that indisposition, ever to consult, or to ask for advice; that love—to put it vulgarly—of having her own way. Anne could well believe that, once the idea was suggested to her, and she had seen its advantages to herself, nothing would prevent her, nothing would stand in her way; and she would be convinced that her daughter, and her family, would view the matter exactly as she did. Anne had had her chance; she had refused it. No consideration of such a thing as waiting for a handsome wedding, or fear of what others would think, would come between her and her ambition. Indeed, she would probably feel that "if it were done, it were well done quickly," for clearly she could place no reliance on Lord Francis's affection, should someone else come along, with a better house, and a few more thousand pounds.

Elizabeth came back into the room, looking flustered. "We are to look after you," she said. "Georgiana and I are to keep you from feeling sad. Come, let us remove to my own room, so that Forrest can clear the breakfast things away, and we can take another look at these papers; perhaps there is some way that you can go to law, and get your fortune back. We will go out as soon as the rain stops; I feel I need a walk, to clear my head. Come, my dear, be assured we will always look after you; whatever happens, Pemberley will be your home."

"I must go out," Anne said. "Forgive me, I must walk now, I must think, I will walk Minette."

"But your piano lesson," Georgiana said. "Mr Lempriere will be here in half an hour, we cannot put the poor man off."

"I will come back; no, do not put him off, but I need this half hour. I pray you, forgive me… no, do not come with me, you are very good, but I must go alone," and waiting only for a warm pelisse, for the weather was chilly, Anne hastened from the house, and made, as always when her mind needed repose, for the stream.

She went there in sorrow, in distress. Yet as Anne reflected, walking there, following the sweet curves of the landscape, something like a curtain seemed to fall away, and she saw a new prospect. She was free! She was rich no longer; Rosings was not to be hers. Walls and pediments fell away, expensive chimneypieces crashed in ruin, formal gardens dissolved, as though she saw them collapsing before her eyes. As for rank, what was it? Rank was nothing without money! *I will not do for poor Sir Matthew, now,* she thought. She had disinherited herself; for she could not for a moment doubt that her letter had helped to influence her mother to such an unexpected decision. She had set herself free!

Running back into the house, she saw Elizabeth. "I will not need Pemberley as a home. I am so happy! Oh, Elizabeth! Do you but persuade my cousin to rent me the little White Cottage, and I will live there and write books!" and she ran off, laughing, to meet her teacher.

Chapter 25

ALL MORNING, THEY COULD DO NOTHING WITH HER. SHE WOULD
have her piano lesson; she played very loud, and the music
rang out through Pemberley like a paean of triumph, however many
wrong notes she played, and there were a good number.

She would not budge from her position. She loved them all, but
she wanted to live alone, and make money by writing. Elizabeth
tried hard to reason with her. It was all very well to talk of living
alone, she said, but Anne had spent all her life in a great house; she
had no idea of the business of housekeeping in a small one. She did
not know what anything cost; she did not know the price of sugar, or
of beef. "I can learn," said Anne. Three hundred and eighty pounds
a year was very little, and would she not need a person to cook for
her, and someone to do the washing, and someone to clean the little
house? She could not do those things for herself. "Yes," said Anne,
"but I should not need a carriage, or a butler, or a footman in livery;
think how cheaply I could live! And I ought to be able to earn a
little money by writing—some people earn a great deal."

"You do not know that."

"Only think, dearest Elizabeth—every guest outstays their
welcome in the end, everyone becomes tiresome after a while. You

do not want me living at Pemberley for the rest of your lives. I am sure my cousin will still allow me the use of his library, and that is all I should ask—that, and to be an aunt to Lewis."

"Lewis will be very fortunate to have such an aunt, but I do not see why you should not still go to London. Seven thousand pounds is a very reasonable dowry, you are very pretty, and pretty girls often marry with nothing, or next to nothing."

"Yes, look at your sister and yourself. But consider, Elizabeth, what a huge sum it would cost me, to equip myself with gowns, and pelisses, hats, gloves, and stockings, and dancing shoes, all the things that girls' families fit them out with, when they go to London! for my mother would give me nothing, now. I must use up a year's income, nay, a great deal more. My cousin has taught me well; I understand what income is, and interest, and capital, and I know that one should never make inroads into one's capital. If it were all for nothing, if I did not find someone I liked for a husband, I should have so much the less to live on. I do not know," she said musingly, "whether I could sell my jewellery, or whether it belongs to my mother. I think the pearls must be mine, for my father gave them to me, when I was quite small, but for the rest, truly I do not know. The lawyers might well write, and tell me to give them back."

"But why could she not do it? Why can she not live alone?" Georgiana asked, while Anne was out of hearing. "I would not stop loving her; whatever home I had, she would be welcome there."

"I know she would," Elizabeth said, "and she would be welcome here, because we know her; but it would not be well for her to flout society's usages in such a way. She would have no other friends, no society; people would not receive her. Our house would always be open to her, but people would not wish to meet her here. You know eccentrics are only acceptable if they are exceedingly rich. Think of Lady Louisa; what would she say?"

"She would not be pleased; she would say that poor Anne had run mad."

"Exactly. And Georgiana, it is one thing for a woman to write fiction, for pleasure, and have her stories enjoyed by her immediate family and acquaintance. But if she be known to make money, real money, by it, she immediately loses some of the character of a gentlewoman, and declines into the number of those who must work for a living: governesses, and paid companions, and such. Yes, there are such people as Miss Burney, and Mrs Thrale, but they are very few, a distinguished minority, and even so, not everyone wishes to know them. Unless Anne's writing became equally famous, she would be shunned and slighted, and although we enjoy her stories, we cannot be sure that she ever would achieve such eminence."

"But," said Georgiana, "by making her mother disown her, Anne has achieved something she has always wanted, and that is independence; and I do not believe she will give it up."

"I know, but oh! Georgiana, I do not want to see her wither into an old maid. She should be married, she should have a husband and children to love. I cannot bear the thought of her living alone, with only her dog for company. Think of poor old Mrs Burniside, who talks to her cat, when we go to visit her, as though it were another human being. 'Oh, yes!' she says, 'Tibby and I are feeling the cold very much,' and 'Miss Darcy is a kind young lady, is she not, Tibby? to enquire after us.' And if you ask her a question, she says 'What do you think, Tibby?' Oh! I should not mock her. But poor Mrs Burniside is a little eccentric; surely Anne would not become like that?"

"I hope not, indeed; no! I am sure that she would not. But loneliness is very bad for people. Anne already begins to regard Minette as a friend, almost human, rather than a pet, and if she were to be too much alone..." Georgiana was so much overcome by such a lamentable prospect that she could not keep the tears from her eyes, and had to hide her face, so that Anne, coming into the room at that moment, should not see.

A little after noon, when Darcy came back, Anne was in the library, writing. The news was all over the country, he said, for everyone had seen the newspaper, and everyone wanted to know whether Miss de Bourgh would stay at Pemberley, or go to live with Dukes and Duchesses, and marry a Lord, at the very least.

His wife told him of Anne's ambition; could they rent her the cottage? Could she live in it, alone? "Certainly not, impossible," he said.

"Well, I do not know," Elizabeth said. "With any other young woman, I would say so. But it is a very unusual situation, and she is a very unusual girl."

"All will be well, you will see; only wait a few days." And he would say no more.

But once she was alone in the library, Anne had to give way to the question that was uppermost in her mind, all the time. What would Edmund think about it? Would his mother write and tell him? How long did it take for a letter to get to the West Indies? if indeed he were there, and she did not even know whether he had arrived.

If only she could get on her horse, and ride, ride straight up the hillside, to his home, and find out! But that was impossible. Could she, on some excuse, go into Burley, and perhaps visit his parents? Every kind of fantastic idea presented itself: she should make believe that she was ill, and must go to the warm bath; perhaps there was some shopping that could only be done in

Burley; the bookshop; maybe there was an assembly—but no! he never went to assemblies. Oh, but of course—he was not there! She was becoming foolish! Well, she would not wait until he came back; she would sell her pearls and get on a ship, and go to Barbados! But she did not know what he thought, or how he felt, it was all conjecture; one could not ask a man a question, on a conjecture: "I am free of my wealth; will you marry me, here or in Barbados?" The very thought made her blush. Indeed, no woman could ask a man any question; women must wait, in silence, to be sought out, to be asked.

In short, the confusion of her thoughts echoed the confusion of her feelings. All she could do, she decided, was to provide herself with a way of living, and wait: If Edmund never came back, if he did not want her, she would marry no one.

In the end, she thought that to do nothing would be cowardly. She took the best alternative that had occurred to her, in an hour of hard thinking. She packed up the manuscript of her novel; it was not nearly finished, the end was merely sketched, but this was not the time to quibble. She addressed it to Mrs Caldwell, and wrote a letter:

She had already been planning, she said, to publish her work, but her situation had changed, as they would probably have realized on seeing the notice of her mother's re-marriage. Her circumstances were much reduced, she was planning to live independently, and she wanted to know whether some money could be made from publication of her writing. Would Mr and Mrs Caldwell "and any other interested person" oblige her by reading the manuscript, and giving their opinions as to whether it would appeal to the reading public; and if so, whether there were any changes that ought to be made?

It was the best she could think of, it must do; and after all it was perfectly true—she did need to find out whether anyone would pay money for her book, for her cousin Darcy had warned her, when she mentioned Mrs Endicott's letter to him, that sometimes publishers paid very little, or wanted the author to pay the costs of printing.

Mrs Caldwell would certainly write to her son, sometime or other: Edmund would know of her situation. She would not feel comfortable until Edmund knew. Why? What did it matter to her? She did not know. Whether he would do anything, what he might do, or how long it would take him, she could not imagine. All that mattered was that she had done all that she could.

The package was made up; she took it to the butler, and arranged for it to be sent. It struck her that, in the future, in the little cottage, there would be no Forrest, and no servant to take things to the post for her. Well! She had done it, when she was first in Burley with her mother; she had got to the post office, and then she was ill and alone. She could do it again; and she would.

"Come, Minette!" and she was off again, along the end of the terrace, past the formal grounds, and toward the stream. Edmund had been right about Minette: in the past few weeks since she had owned the dog, Anne had become a very good walker. She was healthier, and stronger, and now she seemed impelled by some new energy. The little dog, released from its leash, ran ahead of her. The path climbed, she went up, past pools and waterfalls, past rowan trees and limestone rocks, up and further up; she had never climbed so high! The ground grew steep, she had reached a dark, cavernous place, where the stream fell off a high rock, almost a cliff. Moss and delicate ferns grew there, the ground was always damp; the path went no higher; she turned back, and saw the whole of the valley spread out before her in a blaze of sunshine.

As she began to make her way down, stepping carefully on the wet ground, she saw that someone was coming up the path toward her. It was a man, she thought—yes! it was certainly a man. Visitors never came so far; it might be one of the gardeners; but she could see a gentleman's hat, and a brown coat; it must be her cousin, or a visitor. She came further down; the unknown man came up; a turn of the path revealed him to her. It was Edmund Caldwell.

Chapter 26

WHEN PEOPLE AS MUCH IN LOVE AS THESE TWO MEET IN SUCH scenery and such circumstances, they cannot be long in reaching an understanding. Before a quarter of an hour had passed, Edmund had asked Anne to marry him, and she had said "yes."

It was exactly as she had thought: he had fallen as deeply in love with her as she with him, and, they were delighted to discover, at precisely the same moment: when they had smiled together, over the little blue dish.

"But I did not know it," she said.

"Neither did I. I thought it only friendship, and admiration, until I found you in distress over the money from your father's will. Then I knew. But what could I do, other than what I did? I could not allow myself to see you again, until today."

And why had he decided to leave for Barbados? Again, it was as Anne had suspected. Even before the Duchess and her brother visited Pemberley, they had been discussing the possibility of a marriage with Lady Catherine's unknown daughter. Lord Francis's voice was extremely loud, and the Duchess's hardly less so. Naturally, in their hired lodgings, everything they'd said had been overheard. They had been interested, yet puzzled; Lady Catherine had seemed to be half eager for the match, and yet in no hurry; there had seemed to be some hesitation. They had thought Anne might be ugly, or deformed, or stupid. As soon as they had been to Pemberley, and had seen her, and knew that she was a pretty, lively young woman, *his* only question was, how much money he might obtain with her.

The Duchess had urged her brother to press on, and marry Anne, for she was bound to have thirty thousand pounds, let alone what she would eventually inherit. He objected that his debts were so large, and his way of life so expensive, thirty thousand pounds would hardly be enough, and the mother would give her no more, and might live forever. But she had persisted, and got him to agree. Every servant in the place had known about it; and soon the whole of Burley knew that Lord Francis was to marry the young lady who was staying at Pemberley. Then Edmund had met them in the street: "I know, we were arm in arm, and laughing," said Anne. "I was never so mortified in the whole of my life; and you cannot imagine how stupid his conversation was."

"That settled it for me," said Edmund. "Gossip I could ignore—at least, I could try, I could remind myself that it was only rumour; but this seemed like proof, irrefutable proof. All I wanted was to be gone, to be out of England before your marriage took place. But somehow I delayed, and waited, for what, I did not know. Twice I told myself that I could not leave; I turned back because there was some question at work, something only I could deal with. Then I was advised not to go, for the ship would run directly into the hurricane season. This week, I was really going. Tomorrow was the date set for me to leave; and the end of the week for the ship to depart."

"But how did you come here? Did you know about all this? Or did you come to say farewell?" were Anne's next questions. The answer astonished her. It was her cousin Darcy who, on leaving

Pemberley that morning, had ridden directly to his friend's home, and told him of Lady Catherine's marriage and Anne's changed circumstances. Darcy knew that Edmund's journey had been twice delayed, but understood that now he was really on the point of leaving; that his passage was taken; that by the following day, or the day after, he would be gone.

Her cousin had made it clear that, for his part, he considered Anne released from every obligation to a parent who had rejected, abandoned, and insulted her. For him, the offer of the Reverend Mr Whiley was the final straw, an insult to a woman of Anne's rank, abilities, and talents. He knew that his friend was a far better match for her. He felt that there was now no bar to their marriage, if Edmund still wished it. He was to feel under no obligation, however; Anne would always have a home at Pemberley; he and his wife regarded her as a beloved sister. Hearing that his departure was not imminent, he had urged him to take the rest of the day, and consider.

"Then he left. I had hardly taken it in, except that they had offered you some ancient clergyman to marry, and you were to copy out his manuscripts, and that you had said no. I should think so indeed! But as soon as he had gone, I found that I did not need a day to think it over, or even an hour. You were no longer the wealthy heiress of Rosings; you were the woman I love, you had been hurt, you were in trouble. There was nothing to think about." (At this point the relation of the story was somewhat interrupted, as Anne responded to this wonderful declaration.) He resumed: He had called for his horse, and arrived barely half an hour behind Darcy. "Then," he said, "when I arrived at the house, I found your cousin and Mrs Darcy in a terrible state, for, they told me, Anne would talk of nothing but living on her own in a cottage, and writing books.

And I told them that that was nonsense, for you are going to live with me, and write books."

Oh! thought Anne, *I must rescue my package, from Forrest,* and she wondered whether she could tell him of her desperate, foolish stratagem, but just at that moment Edmund began saying such very affectionate things to her that she could not do anything, except smile up at him, with tears in her eyes, and assure him that she felt just the same!

Some people might have been surprised at the length of time it took for the two of them to return from what had been, really, quite a short walk; but Elizabeth and Darcy were not of their number. They had too recently been in a similar situation themselves. "You are going to be as happy as we are," Elizabeth said. "I did not think it possible, but I believe you will manage it."

But, as she later told her husband, even she had not such reasons for delight as Anne had, in the contrast between her earlier life, and the life that lay ahead of her. "If my mother was sometimes peevish, and my father occasionally morose, I had all the cheerful society of my sisters, especially dear Jane," she said.

"And the reassurance of your mirror, to tell you how beautiful you were," said her husband, fondly. "Poor Anne spent so many years as a sickly, plain, lonely girl, that she deserves every day, every hour of the happiness that will be hers."

"And how good it is to think," Elizabeth said, "that we shall not lose her, for she will be only five miles away."

The rest of the day was not enough for the expression of everybody's satisfaction, and happy as Anne was in the delight of her relatives, it required several walks in the gardens, alone with Edmund, to establish her composure of mind, and assure her that she really was, not only going to be married to the man she loved, but totally and completely loved by him.

"And are you really happy that I should write, and write novels?" Anne asked.

"Yes, indeed," he said, firmly. "To my mind, it is a wicked thing for any person who has talent or ability not to be allowed to develop it. I shall insist on your continuing, I shall read all your drafts, and I shall insist that household cares never prevent you from having all the time you need."

That evening, she thought, was the happiest of her life, and she would always remember it. In retrospect she could not, in fact, remember anything very clearly. Seated beside Edmund, Minette by her side, surrounded as she was by the dear cousins who rejoiced with her, it seemed to pass in a daze, a glow of joy. The only dissatisfaction Anne felt, as she went to dress for dinner, was that she had really spent so very little time alone with Edmund!

The next day brought another source of pleasure, in the arrival of the Caldwells, who were invited to spend several days with them, and whose joy could barely be expressed. Mrs Caldwell, in the course of a long conversation with Anne, admitted that she had known about the matter for some time. Her son had not intended to burden either of his parents with the knowledge of his situation, but knowing him as she did, it was impossible for her not to be aware of his unhappiness, and to guess at its cause, and on her applying to him to tell her the truth, he had done so. She had mourned, thinking there was nothing to be done. "And now, my dear, I could not be happier, and neither could my husband, for you are exactly the daughter we would have wished for." Her only cause for concern was that, as she said, they must wait a few months to be married. "For, dearest Anne, you cannot imagine what kind of a state the house is in, for gentlemen, as I am sure you know, have no idea when anything is dirty, or shabby. But we will see all put to rights."

"And I think," said Elizabeth, privately, to her husband, "that very few young women have gained a husband, by *losing* a fortune, but that is exactly what Anne has done. Who ever heard of such a thing?"

"You are right," her husband said. "But I only fear that she may have done it very thoroughly."

"Why, what do you mean?"

"I scarcely know; but I am not certain how secure her inheritance is."

Chapter 27

THE WELL-INFORMED READER, AWARE THAT "THE COURSE OF TRUE love never did run smooth," will not be surprised to perceive, from the thickness of the pages remaining, that Anne and Edmund did experience some further difficulties.

However, the initial few days of their engagement gave no hint of troubles to come. Then, one morning, several carriages drew up to the front of Pemberley.

"Oh," cried Anne. "It is my dear Mr Bennet!"

Indeed it was, and with him, a handsome, rather over-dressed lady, with a slightly peevish expression, whom he introduced as his wife. Two young women, one pretty, one quiet and rather plain, were: "My daughters, Mary and Kitty." From the second chaise there emerged a very sweet-faced young woman, bearing a strong resemblance to Elizabeth, and a good-looking young man, whom Darcy shook enthusiastically by the hand: "My friend Bingley." But there was another lady, and Anne thought that Mrs Darcy's face fell slightly when she saw her, for this lady, though younger by far than Mrs Bennet, appeared equally peevish, if not more so. Could this be another sister? The extraneous vehicles contained such a supply of nursemaids, valises, and trunks, as may well be imagined, and

Mrs Bingley, hastening urgently to one of them, demanded and received a small baby into her arms. It transpired that the unknown lady was not Mrs Darcy's, but Mr Bingley's sister, who had been quite unable to travel in the same carriage as the infant, owing to her extreme dislike of hearing a child crying.

The new house was ready, Mr Bingley explained, and they were on their way to it. "But you must have received my letter? I wrote to you, I did indeed, a week ago, that we had heard from the builders—the roof and chimneys are repaired, the house is habitable, and as for the new greenhouse, and the pinery, all that, you know, can be seen to far better when we are in residence. I wrote to you, at least a week ago," but no letter had been received at Pemberley.

Not knowing that her family were coming, Mrs Darcy had invited the Rackhams, mother and children, and Sir Matthew and his mother to dinner. "And to keep the numbers even," she said, "I asked Mr Kirkman, too, for now that I am not matchmaking any more, I find that I quite like him."

"Well," said her husband, "maybe we can find a use for him, for we must persuade someone to like Miss Bingley. He is a little older than she, but they might deal very well together."

"How comes it," Elizabeth asked, "that she is here? For I know she does not like me, and I am sure she has not forgiven *you,* for having the bad taste to marry me."

"It seems that Mr Hurst has a sister who must be invited, with her husband, once in a while, and they asked poor Miss Bingley to vacate the spare bedroom for a few weeks, so the Bingleys had to bring her; and unless we can persuade Mr Kirkman to take a fancy to her, I do not know what we shall do. But you need not be concerned, my dear, for I am quite certain that Mrs Reynolds already knows how many people are arrived, and is making arrangements accordingly, and Forrest, too."

"I am quite sure that they have, but I must go, all the same, and assure them both that I am perfectly astonished with all that they have done, and do not know what we should have done without them," and Elizabeth, excusing herself to her guests, hastened away.

By dinner time, a mystery had been unraveled. Mr Bingley, on examining his travelling-desk, had found the letter, addressed and folded, that should have been sent to announce their incipient departure from Longbourn, and the probable day of their arrival at Pemberley. He recalled having no sealing-wax, and laying it aside until he should ask his wife for some. "And then, oh yes, Bailey came about the horses, and I went out to the stable yard with him, and I must have forgot." By this time, however, rooms had been found and prepared for everyone, and in spite of, or perhaps because of, Mrs Reynolds's perturbation, the dinner was all that a Pemberley dinner ought to be.

Afterward they danced. Owing to the shortage of gentlemen, each of the ladies was sometimes obliged to sit down, and after an energetic country dance, Anne was glad to do so. She overheard Mrs Bennet ask Mrs Darcy, "But why is Miss de Bourgh to marry that very odd man? He is not rich, he is not handsome, and you tell me she could have married a Lord."

"Hush, madam, pray hush, she will hear you."

"Oh! nonsense, no one can hear in such a crowd. Well, if such a man as that is to marry into your family, and to be invited here, I do not see why you, and your husband, had to be so very nice about inviting poor Lydia. After all, she is one of us; she is your sister still, and he is your brother, and his brother, too."

"But, the circumstances…"

"Oh, pooh; nobody cares about that; dear Wickham should not have run off with her, but much may be excused to a man in love, and they are safe married now. Lydia is in poor health, for she is expecting an interesting event, as I told you, and their lodging is not commodious or comfortable. I do think it is hard that she is not to come, for a spell at Pemberley, with her sisters, would have raised her spirits, and improved her health. And dear Wickham talks a great deal about his childhood home, and I am sure he misses it very much. Why should you not all be reconciled, pray? If you and Mr Darcy are ashamed of her, you must be ashamed of us, too."

This was perhaps the first time that Mrs Bennet and her daughter had had a serious conversation since Elizabeth's marriage. But Mrs Darcy was no longer the unmarried and not-much-loved daughter, who must treat a parent with respect and deference. She answered with the authority of a married woman, with a home, husband, and child of her own. "I am sorry, madam; but I cannot invite her. For one thing, I do not think she would do well at Pemberley, for you know how noisy and indiscreet she is. But even if I did wish to invite her, it cannot be. I could not ask her without asking her husband, and Mr Darcy will not permit it; he will not receive him."

They moved away, leaving Anne puzzled and surprised. To refuse to invite a sister, who was not at all wealthy, and not well! It seemed so unlike the new, kind cousin whom she had begun to know! She turned and found Georgiana standing beside her. Mrs Bennet, who might, Anne thought, be becoming slightly deaf, had spoken pretty loudly, and she could see clearly, from Georgiana's expression, that she had heard, too.

"You think my brother unkind," Georgiana said.

"I do not understand," Anne said. "It is not like him, or Elizabeth. They are so generous, they have been so welcoming to me, though I am but a cousin and might be thought to have far less claim on their hospitality. It disturbs me that these people seem unwelcome here, because they are poor and of lower rank than I."

Georgiana drew a deep breath. "I can explain," she said, "and I will. I cannot bear it, that you should think my brother ungenerous. But I cannot tell you now. Come for a walk with me, come tomorrow morning; the men will all be out shooting—yes, Edmund too, for I heard him tell my brother that he should go—and we can be private."

Chapter 28

THE NEXT MORNING, THEY WALKED OUT TOGETHER, AND WENT up the stream, whose deep, secluded valley was the chosen spot for every quiet conversation, every confidence. As soon as they were out of sight of the house, Georgiana began: "What I am going to tell you now, Anne, I have never spoken of to a soul," she said. "My brother knows of it, and Elizabeth knows some of it, but no one else. I know I can rely on you to mention it to no one."

"Of course," Anne said. If secrecy meant so much to Georgiana, then clearly even Edmund could not be told.

"This happened a few years ago," Georgiana began, "before my brother was married. Both my parents had been dead for some years, and I was at a school in London. My brother sometimes came to see me, but a young man has not often very much time for visiting a younger sister; and I missed my dear mother so very much."

"My father and I were very close," Anne said. "I know what it is, to mourn a beloved parent."

"When I was fifteen," Georgiana continued, "I was judged old enough, or accomplished enough, anyway. I was thought ready for life, for I could play the piano very well, and the harp a little, and paint, and could speak French and read Italian. No one gave any thought to the fact that I knew nothing of my own feelings, or of my own nature. Since my brother was not married, an establishment was set up for me, and a lady was hired to take care of me: that is, to see to it that I was fashionably dressed, and to take me into company. She was lively and gay, and if some of the sentiments she occasionally expressed seemed not very proper, she was amusing, and I thought it a part of fashionable life. She would tell small lies, and laugh, and recount improper stories—but again, very amusingly, so that the impropriety seemed not harmful, and it would seem prudish to object. Her taste in clothes was excellent; I liked her, though I did not love her; we saw something of my brother from time to time, and I did not think myself unhappy.

"London is not a good place to stay in for long. I began to cough, and the doctor said it was from the bad air, and that I should go for a while to a seaside place. So Mrs Younge recommended Ramsgate; she had friends there, she said, and the place was delightful. She found us some pleasant lodgings, and we began our stay. I had not been there three days, when on coming back from a walk, I was told, 'Somebody to see you, miss,' and there, in our sitting room, was... Mr Wickham."

"You mean... the husband of Mrs Darcy's sister?" said Anne. "Oh, but of course, I had forgot, you knew him well; he was born here, was he not?"

"Yes, during my earliest years he was almost like a brother to me, and I knew him at once, though I had not seen him since he had gone to Cambridge. He came to me and gave me the affectionate greeting of a brother. Anne, I fell in love with him at that moment. He was with us every day; Mrs Younge encouraged his visits. She was forever telling me how much in love with me he was; she had seen it at the first moment; she had never seen a man so much in love; what a pity that my brother, so cruel, harsh, and proud, would never countenance his suit! She advised me on no account to speak of my feelings to my brother, for he would certainly be very angry.

"I thought that it must be true, for Wickham had told me, very sadly, that my brother's former friendship to him was at an end; he did not know why; but he had been promised a living near Pemberley, and when the incumbent died, it had been given to another man. I learned later that his way of life was so dissipated that he was highly unsuited to be a clergyman. But of course I saw nothing of this; his manners to me were unvaryingly gentle, affectionate, and refined; and I believed Mrs Younge's assertion that my brother had changed, and become proud and selfish.

"Anne, I was but fifteen, and had never received such attentions from any man before. All this, and two or three novels from the lending library, were enough to make me see myself as a star-crossed heroine. I was convinced that my life would be blighted forever, unless we were married. Both Wickham and Mrs Younge assured me that there was but one thing to do: to elope. But, she said, she would assist me, she would make every arrangement; and I assumed her to mean that she would go with us, to make everything proper, until the knot should be tied.

"I consented." She paused, and then continued.

"It was a Saturday, and since I did not like the idea of Sunday travel, we were to depart on the Monday. What a scruple to advance, against such impropriety, such rashness, such deceit! But it saved me. The chaise was ordered for Monday. Then I learned, walking into the drawing room and accidentally overhearing their conversation, that she was not to accompany us; I was to go alone, with Wickham. She could not endure it, she said; I thought *then* that she only meant that she could not bear the fatigue of such a long journey. I was shocked; they saw my face; they rushed to reassure me: Did I not trust, Wickham asked, the man I loved? I had given my word; I did love him; but I was frightened, I was doubtful. I could only tell myself that he did love me, and that once the border was crossed, we would straightway be married.

"That same evening, my brother arrived, and cutting short Mrs Younge's gushing flow of greetings and enquiries, requested a private interview with me. In the most affectionate terms, he enquired after my health and state of mind; he told me that he regretted having stayed so long away, and having seen so little of me in London. He asked me how I liked Ramsgate—was I truly happy? If not, a pleasanter place could be found; and did I truly find Mrs Younge a suitable companion? He seemed so different from the ogre who had been depicted to me by Mrs Younge—she must have been mistaken—surely, so kind a brother would not refuse me the marriage I so deeply desired! I began to recall other things—small things, that suggested that she was not always truthful or honest; and I admitted that, in many ways, I did not trust her.

"He told me then that, before leaving town, he had made some enquiries that he should have made before he engaged Mrs Younge, and had learned that she had been for some time the partner, in an irregular connection, of Mr Wickham. There could be no doubt; he had spoken to some people, cousins of hers, from whom they had rented some expensive furnished lodgings, from which they had decamped without paying any rent.

"I recalled all manner of speaking looks, of gestures, of things said, that had obviously a meaning from which I was excluded. The scales fell from my eyes. I was the victim, the foolish victim of a vicious deception, intended to put them both in possession of my fortune, for only the want of money had caused them previously to part, and go their separate ways. If my kind brother had not come when he did… If I had eloped, if I had married him…"

Anne shuddered.

"So you see, Anne, that is why Mr Wickham cannot be invited here; and since he cannot be invited, neither can his wife. I have never set eyes on him since that day. I could not bear it, and neither could my brother."

"But I am glad I have told you this, cousin. I have said nothing of it to anyone, not even to dear Elizabeth. She knows, of course, but we have never spoken of it; and I only mentioned it, because I could not let you think my brother unkind; but telling you has somehow made it more bearable; I do not know why."

Anne said everything she could to reassure Georgiana and tell her how honoured she felt by her confidence. Poor girl! As they walked back to the house, Anne thought of Edmund's honesty, the delicacy and integrity of his behaviour, and of her own good fortune. She could only hope that her poor cousin's heart would soon receive its only proper cure, in the affections of such a man—but where was another to be found to compare with Edmund?

The gentlemen were to return by midday, and it had been agreed that they would all meet in the dining room. She could hear men's voices: yes, they were back. As she hurried to the library, to leave Minette in her accustomed basket, she wondered whether Edmund would guess where she was, and meet her there. As she crossed the hall, one of the younger Miss Bennets came hurrying out of the library, and she recognised the elder sister, the rather plain Miss Mary.

"Oh, Miss de Bourgh," Miss Bennet cried. "I went to look for you, everyone is looking for you. You are to come at once, for they are all in an uproar. Mr Darcy has had a letter, and Lady Catherine has taken all your money away, and they say that you cannot be married."

Chapter 29

M R DARCY'S FEARS HAD PROVED WELL FOUNDED. A SECOND lawyer's letter had arrived, to inform them that Sir Lewis de Bourgh had left the five thousand pounds, which his daughter was enjoying, in trust, only "until such time as she should marry," at which time, of course, he had assumed that a proper provision would be made for her. It has been said that what always happens, after legal provisions have been made, is the unexpected; no one could have envisaged that Anne would marry without her mother's consent or approval. Such, however, was the case: her mother was very angry, and with the entire estate at her discretion, was not prepared to allow Anne anything at all.

Anne was a little surprised to find the entire Bennet family abuzz with the news; she liked them very well but knew them little; it might have been expected, she thought, that Mr Darcy would discuss the news with her and Edmund privately, at least at first; and as she hastened to his business room, she even thought, *What could he mean by such horrible indelicacy?*

"My dear Anne," Elizabeth cried, "we are so sorry!" It transpired that Mr Darcy, appalled by the letter, had dashed into his wife's sitting-room, where she was occupied with her child, and informed her of the whole, giving full vent to his feelings, and unaware that Mrs Bennet was sitting with her daughter, screened from his view by the back of a large armchair. From such a woman, of course, there was no hope of discretion, and the news was all over the house in the course of half an hour.

Mr Darcy's lawyer was hastily summoned: suits and counter-suits were suggested, for clearly it had been Sir Lewis' intention that Anne should have, not less money, but more, on her marriage. "My dear sir, intentions do not matter," said Mr Foreman. "Unless she is feeling charitable, and wants to provide a good living, for some years, for several lawyers and their wives and children, Miss de Bourgh should certainly not go to law, for nothing else would be gained by it."

Everyone had a voice, everyone had an opinion. Mrs Bennet's, expressed only to her daughters, was that Anne was well served for not marrying the son of a Duke; Mr Bingley's was that it was the worst thing he had ever heard, which he repeated until even his wife grew tired of hearing it. Miss Mary Bennet had been reading in the library, and found an old book of household recipes; how it got there, no one could imagine, but it assured the reader that it was possible to live on sixpence a week. Anne felt that this, at least, was an attempt to be practical; and "Look, Edmund," said she, "it says that a very good soup can be made from watercress, which grows in the streams, you may pick it for nothing; and they say that beer can be brewed from nettles."

"I think that nettle beer might make you bilious," said Mrs Darcy. "I think we should find some other solution."

Edmund, taking Anne's hand, declared firmly that he would not hear of breaking the engagement, or even putting off the wedding: he was willing to risk everything, and marry, if Anne were willing; and if they could not live in England, they would go to Barbados. Anne, handfasted with her lover, begged Mr Darcy only to procure them a special license, and they would marry that very day!

At this point, it was insisted by Mr Darcy that a moratorium should be called until everyone's feelings died down, and everybody separated, to exclaim, and advance their own views, and propose their own solutions.

Darcy and Elizabeth did not at all like the idea of their young friends going to Barbados; but Edmund's house, as well as being historic and beautiful, needed a good deal of money spent. Darcy was concerned for the roof, and Elizabeth for the furnishing. "And Anne has had no experience of running a house," she said.

"But you knew very little," her husband said. "Do you not recall your mother saying that only Miss Lucas knew how to cook, that you and your sisters had nothing to do with housekeeping?"

"That is true; but even so, I know more than Anne, for she has always lived either at Rosings, or here, great houses with butlers and housekeepers; as far as she knows, dinner comes to the table, and washing gets done by itself. She must have a capable housekeeper, at least, or she will have a terrible struggle, and it is all very well to say that she can earn some money by writing, but how is she to find the time to write? Especially if they have some children, as I hope they will. But where there are little children to care for, and very little money, a woman has no spare time at all; she is fortunate if she gets a few hours' sleep at night."

Matters went on in this way for several days, with everyone making suggestions, and no one suggesting anything useful, for the fact was that, though his prospects were excellent, Edmund's income, at present, could not be thought sufficient to support a wife and children, as well as his parents. The best advice that anyone could give was that recommendation, so depressing to a lover's hopes, so killing of youth and joy: "Wait."

Chapter 30

SURPRISINGLY, IT WAS LORD FRANCIS WHO SAVED THE SITUATION. He was not a clever man, nor particularly generous, but he was not unkind, and he knew his world. During their short acquaintance, he had liked Anne, and he bore her no resentment for her refusal of him, since he had made a far better match in her mother. Also, he was in an exceedingly good temper.

It had been agreed, as a condition of the marriage, that Rosings should be sold, for "What good does it do for one's standing in the world," said Lord Francis, "to be shut away in the country, when you could live at Stilbury Castle with my sister?" Lady Catherine, delighted at the prospect of living with a Duke and a Duchess, had consented; and a buyer, a rich manufacturer, had been found, and a very handsome price agreed upon, far more rapidly than could have been anticipated. In the course of subsequent financial discussions, Lady Catherine happened to mention that an advantageous saving had been made in the denial of Anne's dowry.

To her astonishment, Lord Francis told his bride that it was a d—d shame. "I don't like her choice of a husband," he said, "but it ain't right to pauperize the poor girl. And don't think it won't be talked of," he added. "People always know; everything gets known.

Girl marries a quarryman, they talk about her. You cut her off without a shilling, they talk about us. Sort of thing that gets in the papers. Don't want that. D_ it, ma'am, I won't have it. Let the girl have ten thousand. I'll see Colby about it tomorrow."

Lady Catherine, on both of the occasions of her marrying, had thought nothing, standing beside her bridegroom, of promising to "honour and obey" with no intention of doing any such thing. Now, for the first time in her life, she actually found herself in a position of being obliged to do something, whether she wanted to, or no; and Anne's marriage was not long delayed.

Anne went to live at the house on the hillside, and the room with the wide-sweeping views was the beloved haven where she wrote her books. The little white cottage became the home of Georgiana's old nurse, Mrs Grainger.

The quarry prospered, and in a very short time Edmund had a quite sufficient income to support a family. Although they never made a large amount of money, the series of historic novels by "A. Caldwell" (publisher: John Endicott) enjoyed a good success with the more discerning members of the reading public.

Anne's impression that she might like Mary Bennet was well-founded. Mary, who had never received much affection from either her two silly sisters or her two clever ones, found a friend in Anne. By suggesting books that she herself liked, exchanging letters, and receiving Mary for the occasional visit, Anne was able to direct her mind, and actually persuaded her, rather than collecting extracts, to try a little writing. Mary wrote some pretty verses, and became more self-confident, and much happier. Her looks improved with the improvement in her spirits, with the result that she and her mother actually began to enjoy each other's company. They lived together with much more of mutual cheerfulness, and Mary, having got a few of her verses published in the kind of periodicals that ladies read, became something of a star in Meryton society, and received the admiration she had always craved.

Darcy and Elizabeth continued as happy as they had always been. Lewis Bennet Fitzwilliam Darcy grew up a beautiful, clever, and sweet-natured child, and had several brothers and sisters, all as delightful as he. Their favourite excursion was to ride their ponies up the track to see Cousin Anne, who read them the most wonderful stories, and spoiled them, their father said, quite dreadfully. The road to Pemberley was never made up for carriages, but that deterred none of them from making the journey very frequently, for Anne regarded Darcy and Elizabeth as a brother and sister, and Pemberley as her second home.

Georgiana had one season in London, enjoyed it very much, came home, and married Mr Rackham; thus becoming happily settled within two miles of Pemberley; and when Minette had a litter, Anne gave her a puppy.

Mrs Annesley, now Mrs Fitzwilliam, was, as her husband had suspected, a perfect soldier's wife. She went with him to every place that he was sent to, could make a home anywhere, in any circumstances, was never dismayed by bad weather, supply problems, or the sound of cannon fire, and was beloved by everyone in the regiment.

As to the happiness of Lady Catherine and her husband, it may be assumed that she reaped the reward of her marriage, in the opportunity it gave her, as the sister of a Duchess, to associate with those of the very highest rank. The happiness of Lord Francis may be inferred from the fact that, soon after they were married, he spent forty thousand pounds of her money to purchase the command of a regiment of cavalry.

Chapter 31

Lady Francis Meaburn to Mr Fitzwilliam Darcy

Stilbury Castle

My dear Nephew,

I was pleased to receive your letter, for it has been quite a period since we corresponded. However, I cannot accede to your request to forgive my daughter, come to Pemberley, and be reconciled, merely because she has given birth to her second child. Nor can I do so for the other reason you mention, to celebrate the publication of her new book. I cannot regard this as a fortunate circumstance, much less a cause for congratulation.

Nothing will ever induce me to countenance her marriage to that stonemason, and I absolutely refuse to meet him. Families like ours do not admit such people to our circle of acquaintances. Anne has betrayed her family by her disgraceful marriage, and she does not deserve to be received or acknowledged. If you choose to do so, I cannot prevent you, but I shall always look upon it as the lamentable result of your own marriage to a woman with no rank, and no money.

As for Anne's writing, I suppose I must be thankful that she publishes under her married name, and has not disgraced the ancient and honoured name of de Bourgh. I have not read any of her books, and do not intend to. If she had published a book of elegant extracts, it would have been perfectly acceptable; or she might have written pleasant little verses, as the Duchess' sister, Lady Augusta, does. But ladies of quality should not write works of fiction, to amuse the idle and the unlearned. Novels ought to be forbidden, for they are only read by women who spend their time uselessly and neglect their duties. I never read, except for the newspaper; I have better things to do, unless for any reason I am not able to go to church, when I read from a collection of sermons by the late Reverend Dr William Grisby, a friend of my late father's. When I have come to the end of the volume, I begin again at the beginning. This has been my practice for thirty years, and I see no reason to change it.

I am residing at Stilbury, as you see; and the poor dear Duchess is with me. The Duke's behaviour is becoming very strange. I can manage him; but she is afraid to be alone with him. I am not betraying a confidence in revealing this to you: everyone knows about it since the incident in Piccadilly, but he cannot be shut up, not yet, at any rate.

I dare say you saw the announcement in the newspaper, of Lord Francis' appointment to the command of the —th cavalry regiment. It is the finest regiment in the Army. The appointment cost a great deal of money, but no other regiment, and no other command, would do for a person of such lofty rank and distinguished family.

Since he was gazetted, Lord Francis has been continuously in London, working very hard in the service of his country. I expect you have seen those disgraceful articles in the newspapers, casting aspersions on his way of life. The wretched people who write these things should be arrested and punished, but it seems they cannot be stopped. He is not a spendthrift, as they say; military life is very expensive; you should see the bills I have had, for hundreds of pounds, and a note with them saying that they are for his uniforms.

He has spent a great deal on uniforms for the men, too, for he likes his troops to look smart, which is very unselfish of him, for if they have to go and get killed, the uniforms will not be returned, and we shall be out of pocket.

It is certainly not true that he drinks three bottles of champagne in an evening; he never drinks more than two, and he quite often visits the troops, or at least the officers, though of course if there is a war, he will not risk his life in the line of battle; why should he? The soldiers do that sort of thing; he will stand on a hill, with a telescope, and direct things. After all, they have not paid for their employment; and if he were killed, forty thousand pounds would be lost.

I still hold the living of Rosings, and I want to put Mr Septimus Whiley in there, for he is excessively tedious and thinks of nothing but his books; the Duchess wants to be rid of him. The Collinses could exchange with him, leave Hunsford and come here, for though Mr Collins is equally tedious, he does show a proper respect for rank, and can be useful in little ways; but Mrs Collins writes that they do not want to move away, only because the fruit trees that Mr Collins planted are beginning to bear! You would think, after all that has passed, that they would be willing to oblige me. But people of that class are extremely insensitive.

Believe me, nephew, I am not dead to all family feeling, and there is nothing I would like better than to come to Pemberley again. If ever you come to your senses, regain the consciousness of your rank, and give up Anne's acquaintance, I shall be delighted to visit you. Until then, I remain, believe me,

Your affectionate aunt,

C. de Bourgh Meaburn.

About the Author

Judith Brocklehurst was more fortunate than Elizabeth Bennet, for she got to the Lakes—in fact she was brought up there, and it was on visits to the magnificent scenery of Derbyshire that her passion for Jane Austen was developed. She won a scholarship and attended Cambridge University, then emigrated to Canada in the sixties with her husband and two young daughters, and worked as a teacher and newspaper columnist. Her greatest pleasure was writing Jane Austen sequels by installments and sharing them electronically with Janeites all over the world.

Mrs. Darcy's Dilemma
DIANA BIRCHALL

"Fascinating, and such wonderful use of language."
—JOAN AUSTEN-LEIGH

It seemed a harmless invitation, after all...

When Mrs. Darcy invited her sister Lydia's daughters to come for a visit, she felt it was a small kindness she could do for her poor nieces. Little did she imagine the upheaval that would ensue. But with her elder son, the Darcys' heir, in danger of losing his heart, a theatrical scandal threatening to engulf them all, and daughter Jane on the verge of her come-out, the Mistress of Pemberley must make some difficult decisions...

"Birchall's witty, elegant visit to the middle-aged Darcys is a delight." —PROFESSOR JANET TODD, UNIVERSITY OF GLASGOW

"A refreshing and entertaining look at the Darcys some years after *Pride and Prejudice* from a most accomplished author." —JENNY SCOTT, AUTHOR OF *After Jane*

978-1-4022-1156-0 • $14.95

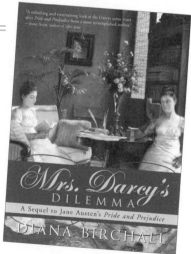

The Darcys Give a Ball
ELIZABETH NEWARK

"A tour de force." —MARILYN SACHS, AUTHOR OF *First Impressions*

Whatever will Mr. Darcy say…

…with his son falling in love, his daughter almost lured into an elopement, and his niece the new target of Miss Caroline Bingley's meddling, Mr. Darcy has his hands full keeping the next generation away from scandal.

Sons and daughters share the physical and personality traits of their parents, but of course have minds of their own—and as Mrs. Darcy says to her beloved sister Jane Bingley: "The romantic attachments of one's children are a constant distraction."

Amidst all this distraction and excitement, Jane and Elizabeth plan a lavish ball at Pemberley, where all the young people come together for a surprising and altogether satisfying ending.

What readers are saying:

"A light-hearted visit to Austen country."

"A wonderful look into what could have happened!"

"The characters ring true, the situation is perfect, the conclusion is everything you hope for."

"A wonder of character and action… an unmixed pleasure!"

978-1-4022-1131-7 • $12.95 US/ $15.50 CAN/ £6.99 UK

Mr. Darcy's Diary
AMANDA GRANGE

"A gift to a new generation of Darcy fans
and a treat for existing fans as well." —AUSTENBLOG

The only place Darcy could share his innermost feelings...

...was in the private pages of his diary. Torn between his sense of duty to his family name and his growing passion for Elizabeth Bennet, all he can do is struggle not to fall in love. A skillful and graceful imagining of the hero's point of view in one of the most beloved and enduring love stories of all time.

What readers are saying:

"A delicious treat for all Austen addicts."

"Amanda Grange knows her subject... I ended up reading the entire book in one sitting."

"Brilliant, you could almost hear Darcy's voice... I was so sad when it came to an end. I loved the visions she gave us of their married life."

"Amanda Grange has perfectly captured all of Jane Austen's clever wit and social observations to make *Mr. Darcy's Diary* a must read for any fan."

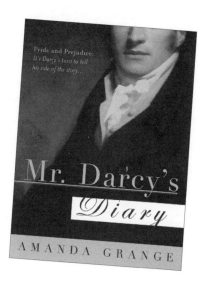

978-1-4022-0876-8 • $14.95 US/ $19.95 CAN/ £7.99 UK

Mr. and Mrs. Fitzwilliam Darcy: Two Shall Become One

SHARON LATHAN

"Highly entertaining... I felt fully immersed in the time period. Well done!" —*Romance Reader at Heart*

A fascinating portrait of a timeless, consuming love

It's Darcy and Elizabeth's wedding day, and the journey is just beginning as Jane Austen's beloved *Pride and Prejudice* characters embark on the greatest adventure of all: marriage and a life together filled with surprising passion, tender self-discovery, and the simple joys of every day.

As their love story unfolds in this most romantic of Jane Austen sequels, Darcy and Elizabeth each reveal to the other how their relationship blossomed from misunderstanding to perfect understanding and harmony, and a marriage filled with romance, sensuality and the beauty of a deep, abiding love.

What readers are saying:

"This journey is truly amazing."

"What a wonderful beginning to this truly beautiful marriage."

"Could not stop reading."

"So beautifully written...making me feel as though I was in the room with Lizzy and Darcy...and sharing in all of the touching moments between."

978-1-4022-1523-0 • $14.99 US/ $15.99 CAN/ £7.99 UK

Loving Mr. Darcy: Journeys Beyond Pemberly
SHARON LATHAN

"A romance that transcends time." —*The Romance Studio*

Darcy and Elizabeth embark on the journey of a lifetime

Six months into his marriage to Elizabeth Bennet, Darcy is still head over heels in love, and each day offers more opportunities to surprise and delight his beloved bride. Elizabeth has adapted to being the Mistress of Pemberley, charming everyone she meets and handling her duties with grace and poise. Just when it seems life can't get any better, Elizabeth gets the most wonderful news. The lovers leave the serenity of Pemberley, traveling through the sumptuous landscape of Regency England, experiencing the lavish sights, sounds, and tastes around them. With each day come new discoveries as they become further entwined, body and soul.

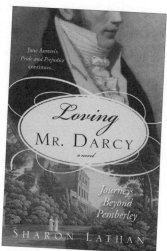

What readers are saying:

"Darcy's passion for love and life with Lizzy is brought to the forefront and captured beautifully."

"Sharon Lathan is a wonderful writer… I believe that Jane Austen herself would love this story as much as I did."

"The historical backdrop of the book is unbelievable—I actually felt like I could see all the places where the Darcys traveled."

"Truly captures the heart of Darcy & Elizabeth! Very well written and totally hot!"

978-1-4022-1741-8 • $14.99 US/ $18.99 CAN/ £7.99 UK

The Pemberley Chronicles

A Companion Volume to Jane Austen's Pride and Prejudice

The Pemberley Chronicles: Book 1

REBECCA ANN COLLINS

"A lovely complementary novel to Jane Austen's *Pride and Prejudice*. Austen would surely give her smile of approval."
—BEVERLY WONG, AUTHOR OF *Pride & Prejudice Prudence*

The weddings are over, the saga begins

The guests (including millions of readers and viewers) wish the two happy couples health and happiness. As the music swells and the credits roll, two things are certain: Jane and Bingley will want for nothing, while Elizabeth and Darcy are to be the happiest couple in the world!

Elizabeth and Darcy's personal stories of love, marriage, money, and children are woven together with the threads of social and political history of England in the nineteenth century. As changes in industry and agriculture affect the people of Pemberley and the surrounding countryside, the Darcys strive to be progressive and forward-looking while upholding beloved traditions.

"Those with a taste for the balance and humour of Austen will find a worthy companion volume."
—*Book News*

978-1-4022-1153-9 • $14.96 US/ $17.95 CAN/ £7.99 UK

The Women of Pemberley

The acclaimed **Pride** and **Prejudice** *sequel series*
The Pemberley Chronicles: Book 2

REBECCA ANN COLLINS

"Yet another wonderful work by Ms. Collins."
—BEVERLY WONG, AUTHOR OF *Pride & Prejudice Prudence*

A new age is dawning

Five women—strong, intelligent, independent of mind, and in the tradition of many Jane Austen heroines—continue the legacy of Pemberley into a dynamic new era at the start of the Victorian Age. Events unfold as the real and fictional worlds intertwine, linked by the relationship of the characters to each other and to the great estate of Pemberley, the heart of their community.

With some characters from the beloved works of Jane Austen, and some new from the author's imagination, the central themes of love, friendship, marriage, and a sense of social obligation remain, showcased in the context of the sweeping political and social changes of the age.

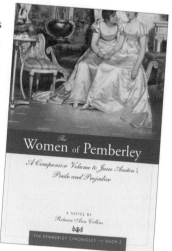

"The stories are so well told one would enjoy them even if they were not sequels to any other novel."
—*Book News*

978-1-4022-1154-6 • $14.96 US/ $17.95 CAN/ £7.99 UK

Netherfield Park Revisited

The acclaimed Pride and Prejudice *sequel series*
The Pemberley Chronicles: Book 3

REBECCA ANN COLLINS

"A very readable and believable tale for readers
who like their romance with a historical flavor." —*Book News*

Love, betrayal, and changing times for the Darcys and the Bingleys

Three generations of the Darcy and the Bingley families evolve against a backdrop of the political ideals and social reforms of the mid-Victorian era.

Jonathan Bingley, the handsome, distinguished son of Charles and Jane Bingley, takes center stage, returning to Hertfordshire as master of Netherfield Park. A deeply passionate and committed man, Jonathan is immersed in the joys and heartbreaks of his friends and family and his own challenging marriage. At the same time, he is swept up in the changes of the world around him.

Netherfield Park Revisited combines captivating details of life in mid-Victorian England with the ongoing saga of Jane Austen's beloved *Pride and Prejudice* characters.

"Ms. Collins has done it again!" —BEVERLY WONG, AUTHOR OF *Pride & Prejudice Prudence*

978-1-4022-1155-3 • $14.95 US/ $15.99 CAN/ £7.99 UK

The Ladies of Longbourn

The acclaimed Pride and Prejudice *sequel series*

The Pemberley Chronicles: Book 4

REBECCA ANN COLLINS

"Interesting stories, enduring themes, gentle humour, and lively dialogue." —*Book News*

A complex and charming young woman of the Victorian age, tested to the limits of her endurance

The bestselling *Pemberley Chronicles* series continues the saga of the Darcys and Bingleys from Jane Austen's *Pride and Prejudice* and introduces imaginative new characters.

Anne-Marie Bradshaw is the granddaughter of Charles and Jane Bingley. Her father now owns Longbourn, the Bennet's estate in Hertfordshire. A young widow after a loveless marriage, Anne-Marie and her stepmother Anna, together with Charlotte Collins, widow of the unctuous Mr. Collins, are the Ladies of Longbourn. These smart, independent women challenge the conventional roles of women in the Victorian era, while they search for ways to build their own lasting legacies in an ever-changing world.

Jane Austen's original characters—Darcy, Elizabeth, Bingley, and Jane—anchor a dramatic story full of wit and compassion.

> **Ladies of Longbourn**
> *The acclaimed Pride and Prejudice sequel series*
> *The Pemberley Chronicles*
>
> A NOVEL BY
> *Rebecca Ann Collins*
>
> BOOK 4

"A masterpiece that reaches the heart."

—BEVERLEY WONG, AUTHOR OF *Pride & Prejudice Prudence*

978-1-4022-1219-2 • $14.95 US/ $15.99 CAN/ £7.99 UK

Eliza's Daughter
A Sequel to Jane Austen's Sense and Sensibility
JOAN AIKEN

"Others may try, but nobody comes close to Aiken in writing sequels to Jane Austen." *—Publishers Weekly*

A young woman longing for adventure and an artistic life...

Because she's an illegitimate child, Eliza is raised in the rural backwater with very little supervision. An intelligent, creative, and free-spirited heroine, unfettered by the strictures of her time, she makes friends with poets William Wordsworth and Samuel Coleridge, finds her way to London, and eventually travels the world, all the while seeking to solve the mystery of her parentage. With fierce determination and irrepressible spirits, Eliza carves out a life full of adventure and artistic endeavor.

"Aiken's story is rich with humor, and her language is compelling. Readers captivated with Elinor and Marianne Dashwood in *Sense and Sensibility* will thoroughly enjoy Aiken's crystal gazing, but so will those unacquainted with Austen." *—Booklist*

"...innovative storyteller Aiken again pays tribute to Jane Austen in a cheerful spinoff of *Sense and Sensibility.*" *—Kirkus Reviews*

978-1-4022-1288-8 • $14.95 US/ $15.99 CAN

Mansfield Park Revisited

A Jane Austen Entertainment

JOAN AIKEN

"A lovely read—and you don't have to have read *Mansfield Park* to enjoy it." —*Woman's Own*

It's not so easy to keep scandal at bay...

After Fanny Price marries Edmund Bertram, they depart for the Caribbean, and Fanny's younger sister Susan moves to Mansfield Park as Lady Bertram's new companion. Surrounded by the familiar cast of characters from Jane Austen's original, and joined by a few charming new characters introduced by the author, Susan finds herself entangled in romance, surprise, scandal, and redemption.

Joan Aiken's diverting tale vividly imagines how the Crawfords might have turned out, and Jane Austen's moral tale takes new directions—with an unexpected and somewhat controversial ending.

"Her sense of time and place is impeccable." —*Publishers Weekly*

"An excellent sequel...remarkably effective and very funny." —*Evening Standard*

978-1-4022-1289-5 • $14.95 US/ $15.99 CAN

Mr. Darcy Takes a Wife

LINDA BERDOLL

The #1 best-selling Pride and Prejudice sequel

"Wild, bawdy, and utterly enjoyable." —*Booklist*

Hold on to your bonnets!

Every woman wants to be Elizabeth Bennet Darcy—beautiful, gracious, universally admired, strong, daring and outspoken—a thoroughly modern woman in crinolines. And every woman will fall madly in love with Mr. Darcy—tall, dark and handsome, a nobleman and a heartthrob whose virility is matched only by his utter devotion to his wife. Their passion is consuming and idyllic—essentially, they can't keep their hands off each other—through a sweeping tale of adventure and misadventure, human folly and numerous mysteries of parentage. This sexy, epic, hilarious, poignant and romantic sequel to *Pride and Prejudice* goes far beyond Jane Austen.

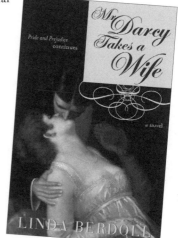

What readers are saying:

"I couldn't put it down."

"I didn't want it to end!"

"Berdoll does Jane Austen proud! ...A thoroughly delightful and engaging book."

"Delicious fun... I thoroughly enjoyed this book."

"My favorite *Pride and Prejudice* sequel so far."

978-1-4022-0273-5 • $16.95 US/ $19.99 CAN/ £9.99 UK